# UNFINISHED NOVELS

# CHARLOTTE BRONTË

## UNFINISHED NOVELS

ALAN SUTTON PUBLISHING LIMITED
in association with
THE BRONTË SOCIETY

First published in this edition in the United Kingdom in 1993
Alan Sutton Publishing Limited
Phoenix Mill · Far Thrupp · Stroud · Gloucestershire · GL5 2BU

First published in this edition in the United States of America in 1993
Alan Sutton Publishing Inc. · 83 Washington Street · Dover · NH 03820

Reprinted 1995

'The Story of Willie Ellin' first published in *Transactions*, Vol. 9, The Brontë Society.
'Ashworth', edited with notes by Melodie Monohan, was first published in *Studies in Philology*,
Vol. LXXX, No. 4, Fall 1983; copyright © 1983 by the University of North Carolina Press.
'The Moores' first published by Hodder and Stoughton, 1902. 'Emma' first published in the
*Cornhill Magazine*, with an introduction by William M. Thackeray, April 1860.

British Library Cataloguing in Publication Data

> Brontë, Charlotte
> Unfinished Novels. – New ed. – (Pocket Classics)
> I. Title  II. Series
> 823.8 [F]
>
> ISBN 0-7509-0481-X

Library of Congress Cataloging in Publication Data

Brontë, Charlotte, 1816–1855.
[Novels. Selections]
The unfinished novels / Charlotte Brontë.
    p. cm.
Includes bibliographical references.
Contents: The story of Willie Ellin – Ashworth – The Moores – Emma.
ISBN 0-7509-0481-X : £3.99
1. Unfinished books. I. Title.
PR4166 1993b
823'.8–dc20                                          93-26286
                                                     CIP

*Cover picture: detail from* Dressed to kill *by Charles Robert Leslie (photograph Fine Art Photographic
Library Ltd)*

Typeset in 9/10 Bembo.
Typesetting and origination by
Alan Sutton Publishing Limited.
Printed in Great Britain by
The Guernsey Press Company Limited,
Guernsey, Channel Islands.

# CONTENTS

# INTRODUCTION

The four fragmentary stories assembled here are interesting for
students of Charlotte Brontë's life and works. When Mrs
Gaskell wrote her biography she mentioned the existence of a
body of unpublished work, but was fairly contemptuous of it.
The manuscript of 'Emma' was acquired by Sir James Kay
Shuttleworth in 1856 and was published in 1860 with an
introduction by Thackeray in the *Cornhill Magazine*. Most of
the remaining unpublished poems and stories stayed in the
possession of Charlotte's husband, Arthur Nicholls, who
towards the end of his life surrendered them into the hands of
C.K. Shorter and his friend T.J. Wise. Shorter and Wise edited
some of the stories, but the pair was also responsible for
dispersing the manuscripts widely. In the twentieth century the
Brontë juvenilia were published piecemeal, and only now under
the editorship of Dr Christine Alexander are they receiving
complete and scholarly treatment. In spite of this, biographers
and critics have been keen to use the juvenilia as evidence for
Brontë's life and keen to trace resemblances between the
juvenilia and the adult novels. Much of this enthusiasm is
misplaced since there is a wide gap between the aristocratic
fantasies of the juvenilia set in the imaginary realm of Angria,
and the humble and sober reality of life at Haworth Parsonage;
it is also unfair to the mature novels to link them too closely
with the incoherent outpourings of Brontë's youth, not
intended for publication.

The four stories here, although never completed or revised
for publication, are in a slightly different category from the
juvenilia. Charlotte had come of age in 1837, and more
importantly had bidden farewell to the burning clime of Angria
in 1839. 'Ashworth', written between 1840 and 1841, marks a

deliberate attempt to adapt the world of Angria to a realistic setting. Alexander Ashworth is the Angrian villain Alexander Percy translated into a disreputable Yorkshire squire, and there are other obvious Angrian names and characters like General West, who have undergone a similar transformation. But 'Ashworth' with its two brothers, Edward and William, also prefigures Charlotte's first full length novel, *The Professor*, where Edward and William Crimsworth are met in the opening chapters in circumstances similar to those of the young Ashworths. Later in *The Professor* the scene changes to a school, as it does in 'Ashworth', and we see the same rather unpleasant hot-house atmosphere in both educational establishments.

In 1842 Brontë herself went to a school in Brussels and there met M. Heger, who as well as providing models for the heroes of her novels, would also seem to have curbed some of the extravagances of Brontë's style. One of the reasons why *The Professor* is better than 'Ashworth' is that it contains less superfluous comment and less concentration on minor characters. Another improvement is that Brontë does make her hero more humble. The Yorkshire industrial magnates are an improvement on the Angrian aristocrats, but the Brontës moved in neither circle; they did, however, know something about schools.

*The Professor* was completed by July 1846, and rejected by several publishers before it was sent to Smith Elder on 15 July 1847. They too rejected it, but with such a degree of encouragement that Brontë hastened to complete *Jane Eyre* which was immediately accepted, and published on 16 October 1847. She then returned to *The Professor* and made three attempts at a different beginning. One of these is probably 'The Moores', sometimes known as 'John Henry', an undated manuscript but one which does have links with *The Professor* as yet to be published and *Shirley* as yet to be written. As in *The Professor* we have two brothers, one of whom is forceful and married, the other shy, vaguely aristocratic, educated at Eton and surprisingly popular with the ladies. As in *The Professor* William has the Seacombes as his patrons, but they are now less aristocratic, being dissenters. John Henry, revealingly called

Edward at one point in the manuscript, is less harsh to his brother than Edward Crimsworth, although there is still antagonism between the pair of brothers.

By the time we get to *Shirley* the antagonism between the Moore brothers is much more muted, although Robert Moore is still a little overbearing and Louis Moore is a fastidious intellectual. There are other links between 'The Moores' and *Shirley* apart from this resemblance of names and the pair of brothers. The Wynnes of De Walden Hall reappear in *Shirley*, and the behaviour of John Henry Moore to his wife and his lapses into Yorkshire dialect remind us of Mr Yorke in *Shirley*. We have as in *Shirley* drunkenness and dissent, often oddly combined, mill owners and class prejudice, praise of the Duke of Wellington and snide remarks about governesses. As in the first part of *Shirley* there is a comic vigour about the narrative, appropriate to what must have been the happiest period of Brontë's life, the year following the success of *Jane Eyre* and preceding the deaths of her brother and sisters.

'Willie Ellin', the first story to appear in this collection, was written well after the completion of *Shirley* and *Villette*, since the date May 1853 appears attached to the first part of the narrative and the date 22 June 1853 is found attached to the second and third parts. 'Willie Ellin' is the least well known and most mysterious of these four narratives, and probably deserves its prime place for this reason. As we read it now, the story looks more like three separate fragments (parts i, parts ii and iii, and parts iv and v) than a consecutive narrative. Even without this difficulty we are still not sure whether the narrator, an Ellin of Ellin Hall, in part i with a vicious half-brother, is the same as the childish Willie Ellin of part iii. Part ii hardly clears up the mystery. In reverting to two brothers, called William and Edward, Brontë is repeating the theme of the first part of *The Professor*, still unpublished, although she had made one more effort to persuade Smith Elder to take it before re-embarking on the Belgian material in *Villette*. She had also in between writing *Shirley* and *Villette* revised her sisters' works, and there are strange resemblances between 'Willie Ellin' and *Wuthering Heights*. The lonely house, the housekeeper, a brutalized child, a timeshift, and above all the unexpected sadistic brutality seem to belong to the world of Emily rather than that of Charlotte, although an examination of the latter's juvenilia might make these Gothic touches less surprising.

1853 is a rather mysterious year in Brontë's life. It was the year of Mr Nicholls' proposal, rejection and peculiar courtship in spite of this rejection. Our main source for the life, letters to Ellen Nussey, unexpectedly dries up during this period, almost certainly because letters containing remarks less than complimentary to Mr Nicholls were discreetly destroyed. It would be fanciful to see the elderly but irate Mr Brontë in the sadistic Edward Willin or to see in the pathetic but adult Mr Nicholls the waiflike Willie Ellin, although it is a feature of Brontë's courtship that her father's anger was counter-productive and her suitor's misery worked in his favour. Eventually Mr Nicholls won his way. In March 1854 Ellen Nussey was informed of an engagement, and in May the marriage took place, although Mr Brontë caused a last minute difficulty by refusing to give his daughter away, his place being taken by Charlotte's old headmistress, Miss Wooler.

The married life of Mr and Mrs Nicholls is difficult to conjecture. Charlotte wrote brave accounts of her honeymoon and the first months of married life, but one would not expect her to do otherwise. One would not expect Mr Nicholls to interfere with his famous wife's writing, but here there is less cause for confidence. The fragments of 'Willie Ellin' and the incompleted 'Emma' seem to be an unsatisfactory recompense for the two years spent since Nicholls' proposal. He denied that he had interfered with his wife's writing, and no doubt believed his denial. His remark, reported by Thackeray, whose courteous introduction does him great credit, to the effect that 'Emma' repeats material in earlier works, does not show great literary discernment. 'Emma' is about schools like *The Professor* and *Villette*, and about orphans like *Jane Eyre* and *Shirley*. But the school attended by Miss Matilda Fitzgibbon is an English, not a Belgian school, and the poor little rich girl of the story is quite unlike poor Jane Eyre or rich Shirley Keelder.

'Emma' is the only one of these four stories which Charlotte did not deliberately abandon. Sadly she did not progress sufficiently in her narrative for it, as with Austen's *Sanditon* or Dickens' *Edwin Drood*, to be worthwhile to make up possible conclusions. Like Thackeray's *Dennis Duval* it remains a brilliant fragment. It does have certain links with stories in the juvenilia, and both 'Ashworth' and 'The Moores' feature schools in which smart girls are fawned upon by sycophantic teachers. This was a world which Brontë knew well, perhaps even better than Thackeray, whose most famous novel begins with just such a school. Occasionally as in *Vanity Fair* and Frances Hodgson Burnett's novel *The Little Princess* and in the life of Brontë's schoolfellows the fathers of such girls came to grief, as clearly Mr Fitzgibbon with his non-existent address has done. But Brontë's early death prevents us from knowing the outcome of this tale; we do not even know whether Matilda Fitzgibbon or the adult generation of Mr Ellin, resurrected from the previous story, would provide the focus of attention.

The text of all these stories is taken from the cited sources. An examination of the widely scattered manuscripts would provide improved or variant readings. The Clarendon edition of *Shirley* gives a scholarly rendering of 'The Moores' and Dr Monahan's admirable article on 'Ashworth' is the basis for the version printed here. The manuscript of 'Emma' is lost; one could make a proper edition of 'Willie Ellin', and no doubt Dr Alexander will do so. This collection is for the general reader who, it is hoped, will appreciate this unexpected insight into Charlotte Brontë's genius.

Dr Tom Winnifrith

# SELECT BIBLIOGRAPHY

C. Alexander, *The Early Writings of Charlotte Brontë* (London, 1983)

C. Brontë, *Shirley*, edd. H. Rosengaten and M. Smith (Oxford, 1979)

C. Brontë, *The Professor*, edd. M. Smith and H. Rosengaten (Oxford, 1987)

W. Gerin, *Charlotte Brontë: The Evolution of Genius* (Oxford, 1967)

T. Winnifrith, *A New Life of Charlotte Brontë* (London, 1988)

# THE STORY OF WILLIE ELLIN

## PART I

I will not deny that I took a pleasure in studying the character of Mrs Widdup, nor that to me she seemed to possess a good deal of worth of a particular kind. Thirty years ago (our acquaintance dated its commencement thus far back) I had believed very heartily in her worth without studying her character. She then ruled me as one of a flock of four – her nurslings. Of this flock I was not her favourite; indeed my place was lowest in her grace. Even through boyhood and adolescence she held me for a riddle rather than a model. After two decades of separation and more than half a generations's change beheld us again under the same roof, still the housekeeper of Ellin Hall, while respecting its master, revolved him day and night as an unsolved conundrum.

It was and must be so: habit and circumstances attached us, but nothing could combine, nothing quite unfold.

In a certain sense Mrs Widdup was spotlessly honest; she had the fidelity of a consistent and steady nature; she was a partisan in friendship, an unflinching foe; she was usually humane and cheerful. She was narrow-minded, loved money, and by natural instinct still leant to the guidance of interest. Fidelity, partisanship, interest, all counselled her to attachment to the Ellin family, and accordingly she was attached to me, that family's surviving representative.

Ellin Hall had for five ages been the home of the Ellins. In my youth it passed out of their hands. My eldest half-brother sold it. He died suddenly, leaving neither will nor direct heir; his fortune fell to me, and I purchased back the ancient homestead. That eldest half-brother of mine was a stronger man in body and a tyrant in heart. I would advert to his deeds, but they are such as we suffer Death to cancel from memory.

## PART II

In other countries, and in distant times, it is possible that more of my kind might have been attracted to human dwellings – hut or mansion – and secretly taken them in lease, than for these hundred years past have been known to make their home in such abodes. Yet we were always few, our presence rare, its signs faint, and its proofs difficult to seize.

My house was not picturesque: it had no turrets, no battlements, no mullioned or lozenged windows. From the first, however, I believe its stones were grey, dug from a grey quarry on a grey waste. They who planned it had loved fresh air, and had chosen a raised site, building it where the green ground swelled highest. Its outlook was free and four-fold: it commanded both sunrise and sunset, and viewed an equal and a wide expanse north and south. These builders, too, preferred solitude to convenience: the village was distant – near enough, perhaps, in summer weather, but remote for a winter's day walk. As to a sentimental peculiarity of the vicinage, I believe the first owners had not known nor reckoned it in their choice of ground. The short, green, flower-bearing turf around covered an ancient burying-ground – so ancient that all the sleepers under the flowers had long ago ceased to be either clay or bone, and were become fine mould, throwing out violets in May, and a carpet of close silken grass all spring, summer, and autumn. These violets were white, and in their season they gathered thickly in a bleached wreath about what seemed a deep-sunk and iron-grey rock – the sole left foundation stone of a forgotten chapel, or the basement of a cross broken away. A quiet gable of the house looked upon this mossy bit of mead. In the lower story of the gable was no aperture, in the upper a single window, having before it a balcony of stone, a peculiarity rare in that neighbourhood, forming indeed the distinctive feature of the house and originating its name – Ellin Balcony.

Who am I? Was I owner of the house? No. Was I its resident tenant, taking it perhaps on lease, and paying the rent? No. Was I a child of the family? No. A servant? No. Ask me no more questions for they are difficult to meet. I was there, and it was my house.

I recollect the first hour that I knew it. I came to consciousness at a moment within the rim of twilight. I came upward out of earth – not downward from heaven, and what first welcomed and seemed to aid me to life was a large disk high over me, a globule, clear, cragged, and desolate. I saw the moon before I could see the sky; but that too, night-veiled and star-inspired, soon opened for me. A sweet silence watched my birth-hour. I took affection for this mossy spot, I stole all through building and nook of land. In the mild beam and pure humidity of a midsummer night I found my seal and sign printed here in dew and there in moonbeam on roof and lawn of Ellin Balcony.

I do not know that ever I was knit with humanity, or was mixed with the mystery of existence as men or women know it. Yet had no mortal relic slumbered near the Balcony, should I have risen? Would Night, my mother, have borne me, unwedded to a certain vital, mortal essence?

Tears had watered this ground; great sorrows and strong feelings had gathered here. Could a colder soil, drenched only with rain and visited only by airs and shadows, have yielded me as its produce?

I even think that some one sleeper threw me out of a great labouring heart which had toiled terribly through his thirty, or sixty, or fourscore years of work, had lived and throbbed strongly, stood still while yet in vigour, and buried, yet warm and scarce arrested, had thrown forth its unslackened glow and ill-checked action in an essence bodiless and incomplete, yet penetrative and subtle.

I believe this because my relations to men were so limited. To millions I felt no tie, found no approach; to tens I might draw gently. Whether units existed that could more actively attract it, yet lay with time and chance to show.

Whoever in my early days were the inmates of Ellin Balcony,

on me they made no impression. I knew every stone in the walls. I knew the neighbourhood – the knolls, the lanes, the turfed wastes, all vegetable growth, field flowers, hedge plants, yellow gorse and broom, foxglove springing bright out of stony soil, ivy on ground or wall. I distinguished and now remember these things very well. I knew the seasons, the faces of summer and winter. Spring and autumn were familiar in their skies; night, day, and the hours were all acquaintances. Storm and fair weather complete my reminiscences. I cannot recall anything human, and yet humanity was in the house. Experience now tells me that it must have been busy, bustling humanity, an alert current of life flowing out after to towns and thickly peopled scenes, returning thence with accessions – life circulating in a free, ordinary channel, never stealing slow under the banks of thought, never winding in deeps, but coursing parallel with populous highways. At last, I suppose, this practical daily life forsook retirement and went permanently away to the towns which were its natural sphere. This departure made no difference to me, except that I remember looking at the sun and listening to the wind with a new holiday feeling of unconstraint.

About this time I first added a cognisance of the individual human being to a vague impression of a human race existing. A solitary old woman became housekeeper of Ellin Balcony. She used to feed a great dog chained in the now empty yard, to close and open shutters, to knit a great deal, and read and think a little. I believe it was because she *did* think, however little, that I had the power to perceive her presence. Those who had lived here before her never thought, and into an existence all material I could not enter.

## PART III

### I

Old Mrs Hill, the solitary housekeeper of Ellin Balcony, was sitting one day in her kitchen reading a pamphlet-sermon as old as herself, when, just as her kettle began to simmer for tea, she thought she heard a noise like the jar of the iron gate opening from a bridle road which approached the lone house. She held her hand, checked her clicking needles and listened. Was it an arrival? It was no more than the wind, which, when it blew as it now did from the south, could rattle that gate like a hand. Sedately superstitious, Mrs Hill, every day and every night, heard noises about this deserted place which scared her, but, firm-nerved, her fears never passed her lips or affected her movements. She passed the jar over and resumed her stocking.

True, there blew a south wind, but in a low key. It shook nothing; it sighed only along the natural avenue which darkened above a path conducting upward from the gate. At this moment the shadow fell not on the path only, but on a small wayfarer — a child's figure — perhaps a little rustic venturing through this gate and up this tree-dark way as a short cut to the bourn of some errand. Is his garb coloured like the path? Does it make a concord with gravel, moss, tree, stem? Are his cheeks and hands berry-brown and red?

Not at all; the shape is less picturesque. It is civilised and slender, a contrast with adjuncts, not a harmony. The dress was made in a town; the hair is long and waved, the face is fair, the countenance is informed. This seems to be a gentleman schoolboy, perhaps ten years old. He must have walked far to-day; he is footsore, pale, and with a few more miles of pilgrimage would become exhausted. He carries a knapsack, a light burden, but his weary shoulder aches under it. Emerging from the avenue, he halts on the little lawn, and looks at Ellin Balcony.

He has measured the house, surveyed the enclosed ground, glanced down into the wooded valley and up at the barer and greyer hills towards which the Balcony fronts. He approaches the door.

The old lonely knitter was winding the worsted round her ball, and folding her knitting, preparatory to taking off the fire the kettle, which now boiled, when the house thrilled to a knock, a loud though brief knock at the front door. She started — and might well start, for it was the first time she had been thus summoned since she kept the Balcony. She ran amazed, she opened, and saw on the step a boy, well clad but dusty, viewing her from under light-complexioned brows with direct clear blue eyes.

'They call you Mrs Hill?' said he.

He was answered affirmatively.

'And this place is "Ellin Balcony"?'

'Yes.'

'If you please, then, let me pass. I should like to come in; I should like well to come in. I'm tired.'

'But, master—' Mrs Hill paused astonished, as if a sudden light broke on her. She quickly pursued – 'Surely you are not an Ellin of Golpit, surely not the little one – the baby?'

'I'm Willie, that is William Ellin, and I came this very day from Golpit – fifteen miles, a long way. I'm tired.'

Mrs Hill let him pass. She took him to the kitchen, and he sat down in a chair that stood on the hearth.

'You *are* the baby, then?' cried the housekeeper.

'Perhaps I was a baby when you saw me. I hope I'm a boy now.'

'How old, Master Ellin?'

'Ten and a half, but I'm a thin boy.'

'You are thin and white. Have you good health?'

'Capital – when they let me.'

'You are like your mother.'

'Am I like mamma? I'm glad of it!'

'You have her mouth, you speak like her. But what, Master William, brought a child like you alone from Golpit?'

'Several things, Mrs Hill. I can't tell you all in a minute – only here I am, and very hungry and tired.'

'Hungry!' echoed Mrs Hill: 'I'm afraid he is hungry,' and she hastened to get a tray and cups.

Before the boy took his tea he asked his hostess to fasten both outer doors of the house. When this was done he said, 'Now I'm safe,' and proceeded to eat with appetite. The meal over, he lay down on a kind of settle. He folded both hands under his head, but did not close his eyes; he was pale but had no look of langour.

'Mrs Hill,' he resumed, 'you knew my mother?'

'I stayed with her in her last sickness, Master Willie.'

'Had she much pain when she was ill?'

'Sometimes she suffered greatly.'

'Was she patient, or not?'

'She was silent when she suffered, and bore wonderfully.'

'She cared for me, didn't she, Mrs Hill?'

'Beyond words,' said the housekeeper. 'And we all used to think you took greatly to your mamma.'

'Well, I suppose it was so. I was not much more than three years old when she died, but I remember her. I have wanted her always, and I shall be glad when I grow out of the habit of thinking about her, as she can never come back.'

'You must have something of her nature in you,' was the reply, 'and I see you have. But I am afraid you have not found many friends, or your mind would not dwell in this way on a dead person.'

'No more it would, I daresay,' replied the lad.

'Do they treat you well at Golpit, Master Willie?'

'I have run away, Mrs Hill.'

'Child, where do you mean to go to, and what will you do?'

'I shall think about it. You must hide me here for a day or two.'

'What has happened wrong? Do they starve you?'

'Oh no, I get enough to eat, but Edward's hand and stick are so heavy.'

'Ah! Mr Ellin never liked either you or your mother.'

-'I believe he was a cruel stepson, Mrs Hill – he still speaks so savagely about mamma at times.'

'And does he strike you, child?'

'If he thinks me slow in the business, which I find dry and hard enough to learn, he knocks my head about till it aches. It is very seldom that I cry, but if I look dull after punishment, he calls me a disaffected rebel, and strikes again. Last night he had been making bargains, and had taken some brandy and water. He knocked me down with a stool, for no particular reason that I know of, unless it is that in some moods he hates the sight of me. My temple was cut with the sharp corner of the stool. I wish, Mrs Hill, you would give me a little warm water to wash it. It is sore and burning now, after my long walk.'

The housekeeper soon brought him a basin of water. She wished to aid him, but he took the sponge himself, and pushing aside his fair brown hair, discovered in the blue-veined temple a rough laceration and dark bruise – it was now darkened with blood – but he soon washed it clean, and then Mrs Hill bound it up carefully.

'My lamb,' said she, compassionately, 'this is wicked work.'

'Old lady, I am not a lamb,' replied the boy, while his eyes laughed. 'And after all it is not so much the knock I think about. I did not run away on that account.'

'What could it be for?'

'Because Edward threatened me with something I really should dread. It seems I am quite in his power, as my parents left me no money.'

'I know, child. Your stepbrother's property came to him in his mother's, your father's first wife's, right. You are dependent on him, as they say.'

'Yes, and he tells me he will bring me up as becomes a beggar – he will make me a shop apprentice. I can't bear it, Mrs Hill.'

The old lady shook her head, and looked somewhat at a loss for a response.

'I can't bear it. I don't want to live with shop boys, and stand behind a counter. My mother was a lady – I ought to be a gentleman.'

'But you've no money; you can't choose. You must learn a trade.'

'We have never had traders in our family for I don't know how long till Edward out of greediness went into business. My father and grandfather and great-grandfather lived here at Ellin Balcony and farmed their own land, and were squires.'

'Yes, and lessened their income little by little. Ellin Balcony would have had to be sold if your brother had not removed into premises at Golpit, and gone, as you say, into business.'

'Would it?'

'Aye; and mind me, you can't do better than follow his example. Would he take you into his own counting house?'

'I should be so miserable.'

The poor lad groaned.

'But, remember,' said Mrs Hill, with much sympathy, but also with deep warning in her tone, 'you are without friends, Master Willie. Edward is your only chance: displease him as little and obey him as much as you can.'

'Can't I go to sea, or be a soldier?'

'You can't – indeed you can't.'

'But Edward is cruel, Mrs Hill; he persecutes me, I think. I don't complain much, I don't tell you all, but indeed I hardly know how to go on living as I have lived for some years.'

'You must look to God – you must, my poor child. It is all that sufferers, whether grown up or little ones, can do in this weary world.'

'I wonder if mamma knows about me, Mrs Hill? I sometimes hope not, lest she should be unhappy in Heaven.'

'Do you say your prayers at night? Have they ever taught you to pray?'

'Yes,' said he briefly. '*They* never taught me – that is, Edward and his wife never taught me my prayers, but I learnt them of mamma, and remember them yet.'

'Don't forget them. Will you go to bed now?'

'Yes, if you please. I'm tired.'

After Mrs Hill had taken the child upstairs and shown him his room, containing a spare bed she always kept dry and aired, he came to the staircase head, and called out anxiously, yet quietly:

'Lock the doors fast, Mrs Hill. Let nobody in, and tell nobody there is a strange boy in the house.'

She promised accordingly.

Worn out with fatigue, he slept till late the next morning. He had not yet risen when the iron gate clashed back and a gig drove furiously up the avenue. In an instant a man athletic and red-whiskered bounded to the yard pavement, entered the kitchen door, and seemed to take house and housekeeper by storm.

'Where is the cub? I tracked him here by sure marks, so let us have no lies. Where is he?'

'Mr Ellin, what can you mean?'

Mr Ellin held up a clenched fist in the old woman's face, shook it between her two eyes, pronounced an oath, and dashed upstairs.

There were seven bedrooms. He tried the doors of six – they yielded. He entered, and found empty rooms. Testing the seventh door, he found that it resisted his hand – a drawn bolt opposed him.

'Run down!' said he. 'I have him now. William Ellin!'

'Yes, Edward,' said a child's voice.

'Open this door!' (Oath accompanying).

'I would open it directly if you would promise not to strike – at least, not hard.'

For answer the great athlete vigorously shook the slight door.

'*I* promise!' he yelled. 'I'll see you,' etc.

Silence within. Again the door was made to quiver.

'If you will not promise,' recommenced the treble organ, uttered in an awe-pierced yet not timid key, 'I must defend.'

'Defend? What do you mean? Open if you value your life.'

'I do value my life, so I shall make a barricade,' was answered, and a dragging sound followed as of furniture moved. The child seemed quietly planning to resist this terrible besieger. Hereupon Goliath foamed at the mouth. Strong hand and heavy shoulder were both made to bear upon the door. It heaved, creaked, swayed. Below knelt Mrs Hill on the landing praying for pardon and forbearance. She might as well have implored stone. Ere long hinge, lock, panels yielded, the whole door crashed in, and thrusting aside an interposed chest of drawers, Edward Ellin sprang upon his young brother. Down went the child before the onslaught, but he got up soon on one knee, and his blue eye did not fall – it rose. Over him flourished the gig whip. He looked at the lash.

'Not too hard this time,' said he in a low voice, inexplicably quiet and steady. 'I have considered, and mean to do my best at a trade.'

The wicked man's arm stiffened its muscles; the cruel lash vibrated, but it did not fall. There was a Providence watching over that poor little Samuel kneeling on the floor in his scant night-shirt.

A voice spoke behind.

'Ellin – not so. I'll not see that done,' declared accents manlier and mellower than those of the husky ruffian. 'Whatever the lad may be, he is not strong enough for the discipline of a gig whip. Let him go.'

The speaker was the second occupant of the gig. Mrs Hill's cries and the breakage of the door had called him upon the scene of action. He looked at this moment a capable protector. He was a handsome man, as powerful as Ellin; and his face, his eye, his voice, attested that by him power would never be abused to cruelty. There might be a certain command about him, but it was unmixed with any propensity to oppress. Many a murderer has owned the light savage eye, the sensual traits, the strong jaw, massive neck, and full red whisker of Edward Ellin. No criminal ever displayed in a dock the countenance, bearing, feature and glance of Mr Bosas.

'Come, Ellin, be calm,' said this last. 'Give me that whip; I'll take care of it.'

The person addressed looked ready to pour out oaths, and indeed forth they rushed, but not on his dark-eyed pleasant opponent. Little Willie bore the brunt of the storm, or would have borne it had not Bosas stepped between.

'Dress yourself,' said he to the boy, speaking sharply but not unkindly. He was obeyed in haste. William meantime still eyed with dread, but no poltroonery, the bull kept at bay by the man. He washed his face and hands too, and as he wiped them on a towel, he looked up at his friend, and said, with a curious kind of resigned endurance, 'After all, sir, do not give yourself too much trouble. I've had that whip before, and shall have it again when you're gone.'

'I hope not,' said the gentleman gravely. 'Come, Ellin, promise me you'll let him off this time.'

Ellin made no promise and gave no answer for some minutes; then, as if his mood had changed suddenly, he burst out laughing, and said –

'Pooh, pooh! I'm only in joke; I'll not touch him. Willie knows me well enough. I'm a passionate fellow, but good-natured.'

'You forgive him, then?' said the mediator.

'Oh, to be sure. I owed the little booby no grudge. Let him play truant no more, and come home quietly now – that is all.'

'Very well. You agree, don't you, my little fellow?' said the dark-faced but kind man.

He spoke without turning to the child. If he had seen him at that moment perhaps the current of his own thoughts might have changed, perhaps an intention might have entered his mind which for the present did not occur to him. But Fate sat in the air invisible at her cloudy wheel. She span on impassive, unravelling no knot in her wool. It was in vain that Willie turned sheet-white, and, for an instant, heart-sick. No man regarded, or could read what a lot the child foresaw. He put neither his thoughts nor his forebodings into words. Prescient but long-suffering, he went back to Golpit that morning.

II

Mr Bosas was no resident at Golpit. He lived, indeed, a great way off in a capital city. Notwithstanding his foreign-sounding name, he was English born, but report ascribed to him a Hebrew origin. There was nothing, indeed, of the Jew in his countenance or eye, yet in his features some of the handsomer lines of Israel's race were perhaps traceable, and might he have worn a beard, curls, rich, dark, and Eastern would have graced his chin.

Between Bosas and Ellin existed mercantile relations, for the former was in business too; and as he was the merchant who bought Ellin's manufactured goods for export, and possessed besides, in his superior wealth and commercial standing, the power of either obliging or injuring to an important extent, Ellin held him in respect, and treated him almost with subservience. Hence the ready concession to his will in the matter of Willie; and for this reason, too, during the two days Mr Bosas continued a guest at Golpit, his protégé remained unmolested.

Perhaps Willie expected this respite would last no longer than the kind merchant's stay; perhaps he wished to express as much; but if so he never found his opportunity to put in a quiet word, nor had he the chance of renewing or conforming an awakened interest at parting. Shortly before Mr Bosas' departure Willie had been sent out on an errand, and when he returned his advocate was gone.

The lad had a small room he called his own. It was only a kind of garret, and contained but a crib and a stool. Yet, such as it was, he preferred it before the smart drawing-room, two floors below. If his poor tossed life numbered any peaceful associations, they were all connected with this cold, narrow nest under the slates. Hither he retired early, on the night after Bosas' departure – rather wondering to himself that nothing had yet befallen him, even dimly conceiving a hope that perhaps his brother for once had sincerely pardoned. It was half-past eight of a summer evening, not yet dusk, consequently Willie had brought a book with him, and sitting near the little window he could read. A year ago some love of reading had dawned in his mind. The taste had not been much cultivated, but it throve on scant diet full as much as was healthful. At present he liked *Robinson Crusoe* as well as any book in the world. *Robinson Crusoe* was his present study.

His thoughts were all in the desolate island, when he heard a step mounting the ladder staircase to his room. It pressed almost the last round ere any more disturbing idea struck him than that it must be wearing late, as the maids – who also lodged in the attics – were coming to bed. Suddenly he felt a weight in the tread which forbade the supposition of a female foot. The wooden steps shook, his door shook too; it opened, and a shape six feet high, broad and rather corpulent, entered.

Willie had never, till now, seen his brother enter his chamber alone by night. In all his trials he had never been visited thus in darkness, and in secret. I should not, perhaps, say in darkness, for the hour was shared between two gleams – twilight and moonlight. It was a very pleasant night, quite calm and warm, and only a few faint clouds, gilded and lightly electric, curled mellow round the moon. The door was shut, the thin child sat on his stool, the giant man stood over him.

'I have you safe at last, and I'll very nearly finish you now,' were the first words, spoken in rough adult tones. None must expect qualified language or measured action from Mr Edward Ellin. He stood there strong, brutal, and ungovernable, and as an ungoverned brute he meant to behave.

The boy pleaded only once.

'Wait till to-morrow,' said he. 'Don't flog me here, and in the night-time. Do it to-morrow in the counting house.'

But his step-brother answered by turning up the cuff of his coat, showing a thick wrist not soon to be wearied. He had brought with him the gig whip. He lifted and flourished it on high. This was the rejoinder.

## PART IV

'Stop,' said the expectant victim earnestly – so very earnestly that the executioner did stop, demanding, however,

'What am I to stop for? It's no use whining – sooner or later you shall have your deserts – you've run away and you shall pay for it.'

'But mind how you make me pay, Edward. A grown-up man like you should be reasonable. That whip is heavy, and I am only moderately strong. If you strike me in great anger you may cut deeper than you think.'

'What then? Who cares?'

'If I were to be more hurt than you think of? If you had to be taken before a magistrate and pay a fine or be transported?' suggested Willie.

The idea was an unlucky one. The whole bearing of the boy was antipathetic because incomprehensible to the gross nature under influence. Mr Ellin growled fury in his throat.

'Insolent beggar!' said he; 'so you threaten me with fines and magistrates? Take that! and that! – & c.'

He had fallen to work. It seemed he liked his business, for he continued at its exercise what seemed a long, a very long time. The worst of it was, Willie would not scream, he would not cry. A few loud shrieks, a combative struggle, a lusty roar,

might probably have done wonders in abridging Mr Ellin's
pleasure; but nothing in the present case interrupted or checked
him, and he indulged freely. At last there came a gasp – the
child sunk quite down – the man stopped. Through the silence
breathed some utterance of pain – a moan or two – the slightest
sound to which suffering Nature could be restricted; but in its
repression only too significant. It induced Mr Ellin to say,

'I hope you have had enough now.'

He was not answered.

'Let me see you play truant again, or wheedle Bosas, and I'll
double the dose.'

No reply – and no sob – perhaps no tear.

'Will you speak?'

The flogger seemed half-frightened, for Willie's exhausted
attitude proved that he had indeed received enough; possibly he
might have swooned, which would be troublesome.

But this was not the case. He spoke as soon as the severe pain
of that last cut permitted him.

'I cannot bear any more to-night,' said he.

Ellin believed him – told him to go either to bed now or to –
another place, whistled and walked off.

By and by, after Willie was left alone, he gathered himself up.
It would have been sad to watch him undress and creep
painfully to his crib, and sadder to read his thoughts. Scarce an
interjection and not a word passed his lips; for some time scarce
a tear wet his eyelashes. He had lain sleepless and suffering for
over an hour ere there came any gush that could relieve; but at
last the water sprung, the sobs thickened, his little handkerchief
was drawn from under his pillow – he wept into it freely – then
he murmured something about his life being very, very hard
and difficult to bear. At last, and after a long pause, he slowly
got on his knees – he seemed to be praying – though there
were neither lifted eyes nor clasped hands nor audible words to
denote supplication – nothing indeed but the attitude and a
concentrated, abstracted expression of countenance, denoting a
mind withdrawn into an unseen sphere, preoccupied with
viewless intercourse. As he returned to earth, his eyes, hitherto
closed, slowly opened. He lay down; probably he believed his

petition heard; composure breathed rest upon him; he slumbered.

Willie cannot take rank as a saint — his patience was constitutional, as his religion was instinctive. Temperance in his expression of suffering was with him an idiosyncrasy. Prayer was a need of his almost hopeless circumstances. Oppressed by man, Nature whispered him, 'Appeal to God,' and he obeyed. Some think prayers are rarely answered; and yet there have been penetrating prayers that have seemed to pass unchallenged all gates and hosts and pierced at once within the veil.

## PART V

The man of bad propensities withdrew. William was left kneeling at his cribside, his face and hands pressed against the mattress. He had been severely flogged, and for a time felt sick, but he was not maimed or dangerously hurt — not corporeally maimed. How his heart fared is another question.

It might seem that the watchful care of God had temporarily been withdrawn from this orphan, as he shrank powerless to resist under a tyrannic hand — as he afterwards moaned alone, pale, faint, miserably though not passionately weeping, compelling himself, according to the bent of his idiosyncrasy, to a sort of heroic temperance of expression, even in extremity of grief. In man's judgment it might be deemed that this child was forgotten where even the fledgling dropped from the nest is remembered. William himself feared as much. There was great darkness over his eyes, and a terrible ice chilled his hopes — his very hearing was suspended. He did not now catch an ascending step on the ladder, nor notice the door once more opening. It required the near glare of candle-light to snatch him even transiently from himself and his anguish.

The hand which brought the candle placed it on the narrow window-sill. Some one then approached Willie, sat down beside him on the edge of the crib; an arm passed round him, another arm drew him towards a warm shoulder, lips kissed his forehead, and eyes wept on his neck.

'Poor boy! Poor wronged child!'

The voice uttering these words belonged to an age not many years beyond Willie's own: the speaker seemed a girl of seventeen, blooming, and with features which, if they borrowed at this moment interest of pity, gave back in return beauty distinct, undoubted, undenied. Fine indeed were the eyes which dropped tears on Willie, and all lovely the arms, the hands, the lips by which he was protected and soothed.

'I heard what has happened – heard it from my room below. I fear you are terribly hurt?' said she.

'I don't care for the pain – my mind suffers the most,' the boy declared with a groan. This sudden transfer from terror to tenderness relaxed for one instant the power of self-control.

'Hush, my love, my child! Hush, Willie, forget him: he shall never hurt you more,' said the young comforter, rocking the sufferer in her arms and cradling him on her breast.

Softened even while relieved, Willie wept fast and free and was soon easier. By gentle hands he was helped to bed, he was lovingly watched till he slept, he was kissed in his slumbers; and then the guardian withdrew, only to think of him through the night, to listen against molestation, and to be prepared at one menacing symptom to come out resolved to defend.

# ASHWORTH

## CHAPTER 1

Long disuse of a pen that was once frequently handled makes me feel as if my hand had lost some of its cunning. Neither can I think with that regularity which in former times seemed habitual to me. I might also complain of an enfeebled imagination for I cannot now, as formerly, call up at will a vivid picture of whatever I wish to see. The desire to regain these powers which seem nearly lost prompts me to try again the task of composition. There is also a certain narrative whose particulars I have often heard from different individuals and which I wish to condense into something like the form of a story, that the names and events therein detailed may not wholly slip from my memory. I have not heard these incidents lately; nor did they come to my ear all at once. Every scene and character to which I shall refer has formed the theme of many anecdotes communicated in the evening talk of sundry homely firesides.

Mr Ashworth was a man much known about the country some years ago. But in the West Riding of Yorkshire where most of his public exploits were performed, his private history remains to this day in a great measure a mystery. In fact, he was a native of the south of England, and in one of the counties, Hampshire, I think, he was known as the head of an important family and the possessor of a large estate. His ancestral residence there was, as I have heard, a picturesque building: large and old, not without the romance of more than one darkly panelled oak room and dignified also with a picture gallery and a stately private chapel. Anybody who likes to take a tour to Hampshire may see it still, though it is sequestered from towns and highroads and deeply bosomed in the woods of a fine park.

Alexander Ashworth Esquire, of whom I am at present speaking, was the son of no very amiable sire. His father was a man infinitely disliked by all his neighbours, high and low, rich and poor. The aristocracy of the county hated him for his extreme arrogance and a certain radical turn which marked his political creed and dissenting bias which characterized his religious opinions. For though he always went to church, he was a professed Unitarian. As for the lower orders, a so severe magistrate and an avaricious landlord could not be expected to be in high favour with them. Yet Mr Ashworth Senior was a man of talent and also of influence. He could always, in case of a county election, bring powerful aid to the side he was disposed to support.

Fractious politicians and men who are bitterly hated abroad are not unfrequently well liked in their own families. I have known them prove kind husbands and tender fathers, as if the sunshine they were so chary of to men in general was poured with fuller and more genial effect on their own narrow hearth and household. It may be said there is a sort of selfishness in this limited benevolence. Be that as it may, Mr Ashworth came in for no share of blame on that score. He was an exceedingly harsh husband and almost an unnatural father. I could never learn that he had good reason to be dissatisfied with his wife. She was an Irish lady of remarkably fine person and generous warm heart, possessed of a cheerful, liberal nature in the days of her youth and freedom, but subdued in the course of her married life to a sedate seriousness of demeanour bordering almost upon melancholy.

What chiefly crossed her were the constant misunderstandings subsisting even from early childhood between her only son, Alexander, and his father. She had no other children; consequently, she thought a good deal about this boy and indulged him much more than she ought to have done. He might have been a self-willed, intractable scamp without this indulgence; he certainly was so with it. And between him and his morose father there was maintained a constant civil war which kept the house in hot water from morning till night.

However, Mr Ashworth fell upon the notable expedient of sending his son to school, not that he might acquire an education, but that he might be out of his sight. He was therefore despatched to Eton, where he stayed till it was time for him to go to college, and, after having taken his degree at Oxford, he came home.

At this time, I believe, he was an exceedingly handsome young man, very tall and *distingué*, considered also to be an accomplished scholar, the truth of which supposition was attested by the university honours which shadowed his temples and thickened over him. He cut a great dash in the county of Hampshire when he returned to Ashworth Hall and was very much admired, especially by ladies. Though a fine fellow as to appearance, he was by no means a good character, and there are sundry tales told concerning him which I have no intention of now repeating, but which involve, in their dark details, names of a softer sound than ought to have been twined with his. I remember two: Harriet, Augusta. To the former, there appertains a sad, to the latter a wild, story. There is romance connected with both and also Sin with her close attendant, Woe. Both ladies are, however, now dead, and the surviving relatives of neither would thank me for disclosing facts which are better sealed up in the urns on their monuments.

Young Ashworth spent a very idle life for some time. At last, his father got tired of seeing him about the Hall, and, after sundry scenes of mutual abuse, tyranny on one side and insolence on the other, he despatched him up to London with orders to study some profession, as he did not mean much longer to be at the expense of maintaining such a dissolute, extravagant rake.

The dissolute, extravagant rake, having arrived in town, proceeded to conduct himself in a manner which showed his fixed intention of meriting the epithets with which paternal fondness had adorned him. In the whirl and change of London life, himself and his deeds have by this time been forgotten there. And yet, I think, there may still survive a few individuals to whom the name of young Mr Ashworth will bring back odd and striking reminiscences. Of course, different persons will remember him in a different light according to the phase in which, at the time they knew him, it was his pleasure to exhibit his many-sided character. Their ideas will also be modified by the cast of their own minds and the comparative extent of their powers to calculate and ascertain character. To some, he will have appeared a very bad young man, too completely the slave of flagrant vice to be capable of appreciating anything good or aspiring after anything lofty; to others, an eccentric and wild being whose oddity was a constant puzzle, sometimes seeming the accompaniment of superior and commanding talent and, at other times, the result of a brain irretrievably cracked. Others again will recognize him by neither of these descriptions but have preserved an image of him in their memories far different from those above hinted at. This class of observers are few in number. I have only heard of two such, and they, it seems, had once set him up as their idol and, like other worshippers of false gods, had doubtless invested their deity with a brightness which was rather the reflected glow of their own imaginations than the natural emanation of the image of clay.

I do not know much of London society, and I can only tell at second hand of the splendid circles into which Alexander Ashworth found admission. Whether these circles were of the highest nobility, I know not, but, by the descriptions I have heard, they possessed at least the magnificence and wealth of aristocracy, if not its rank and titles.

Here, it seems, Mr Ashworth was a star moving in a wide orbit, and not few were the satellites following the planet in its shining track. The young man's accomplishments were varied and some of them, I should think, dazzling or better than dazzling, deeply impressive. With these advantages is crime often connected. Were I writing a novel, I would not have it so. I would select my Sir Hargrave Pollexfen and my Sir Charles Grandison and give inferior talent and bad luck to the former, while the latter should be clad with gifts and graces utterly irresistible. However, I am now speaking of real events, and, as a faithful chronicler, I must say the tale as 'twas said to me.

According to my authorities, Mr Ashworth excelled in music. He seems to have studied and adored the art with the ardour of some frantic Italian or dreaming German. And in society, he often availed himself of his high talent in a way altogether characteristic. He has been described to me as rising suddenly from the centre of a group of ladies gathered under the candelabra of a London saloon and straightway, without speech, making his way to the piano. People were struck and amazed to see the peculiar change which, at such moments, took place in his countenance when he sat down before the instrument and, raising his eyes, which were blue and clear, seemed summoning inspiration from the four winds of heaven. Of course, there was a general hush at such an odd movement, a hush only broken by the deep tones called in full chords from the keys on which Ashworth's fingers fell. I know nothing of music, literally nothing, and I cannot trust myself with any technical terms lest I should commit some horrid blunder. I am imperfectly acquainted with even the very names of musicians and composers. Yet I think I am correct when I say that it was Weber who, having more than once met Ashworth at parties and heard him play, expressed great delight at his performance. I gave this as a sort of warrant for the excellence of what I cannot describe.

When Mr Ashworth played, the ladies would, by degrees, gather round him, and it is said that as the number of his audience increased and the silken rank deepened behind him, his energy or frenzy rose in proportion. Sometimes, my informant said, he would turn and, seeing beautiful faces above and around, plumes and soft curls waving, and eyes all earnestly fixed on himself, he would seem to be thrilled by the power of the moment and bend in ecstasy over his instrument which then answered his touch in such tones as could not soon be forgotten by the dullest ear into which they were poured. Of course, people varied in their opinion of such exhibitions. Some said they were evidences of lunacy, and some, of genius. He did not greatly care which opinion gained the predominance. Whatever impulse took him, he yielded to it, unconscious apparently that his increasing and most eccentric extravagance

might, in time, rather appall than fascinate. Such contortion of
eyes and features might in other faces have seemed terrific or
absurd, but he was very handsome, with a clear, open brow and
a Greek profile- that no twisting could wholly deform. The
presence of ladies did not always restrain his ourangoutang
manoeuvres, and I have heard of his exhibiting himself in the
most infernal style before the very girl he afterwards married.

Her name was Miss Wharton. She was of a Yorkshire family,
a mild, agreeable young woman whose nature one would have
expected to recoil with horror from all that was fierce and
fantastic. Yet fierce and fantastic was the display Alexander
Ashworth thought fit to make one day, in her presence, on the
occasion of some quarrel he chose to pick with Mr Arthur
Macshane (the half-witted but kind-hearted young Irishman
who, through good report and bad report, followed him long
after to the kingdom of his glory). The display consisted in
vehement and overwhelming abuse, preceded, accompanied,
and followed by a series of gymnastic capers, altogether
extraordinary and unaccountable, in which a pair of the longest
legs in England were made to go through evolutions which
would have done high honour to a mountebank but were
utterly disgraceful to a gentleman's son. Miss Wharton and
another lady stood by, astonished and dismayed. When
Ashworth had finished his exercise, he turned to them with a
smile of serene dignity in his face, quite equal to any that
lighted the features of Miss Byron's Sir Charles. It seems to me
that a sort of analogy exists between such scenes as these and the
wild farce of religion which he played on a Yorkshire stage
many years after.

In the full tide of Alexander's London life, he was summoned
back to Hampshire by the death of his father. A natural tie was
thus severed, but, I fear, no natural feelings were touched by
the disunion. It may be questioned, indeed, whether one tear
fell on the grave of that harsh-minded and cold-hearted man,
except what dropped from the eye of his widow. When the
funeral was over, all were glad to forget him. Tenants and
neighbours, shaking off the remembrance of their old landlord,
turned with interest to his youthful son and successor. The first

Sunday after the funeral, he came to church with his mother, and, as he led her up the aisle, his appearance seemed to warrant hopes and expectations which, if formed, were never destined to be fulfilled. He was dressed in deep black, a hue which well suited his tall and slender form and fair complexion. His features were then composed; their beautiful outline could be traced without the interruption of grimace or sneer. An expression reigned over them of solemn and almost mournful thought, and his eye was resigned and lifted. Many people both thought and said that he must be a very religious young man for they never saw anything more heavenly than the aspect of this countenance during the whole service, especially while the organ played.

A week's experience was sufficient to remove the delusion. Scarcely were his father's ashes cold in the family vault and himself fairly installed as master of Ashworth Hall, when he invited down from London three or four gentlemen, the élite of his town acquaintance, whose names I need only record to express their characters – at least there are many now living, in Yorkshire especially, who will not fail from that slight hint instantly to recall the fame or infamy of those distinguished individuals. I allude to Thaddeus Daniels, Esquire, of Castle Daniels, Ireland; George Charles Gordon, Esquire, of Cheviot Lodge, Northumberland; Frederick Caversham, Esquire, of Longchamps, Berkshire; and the unfortunate Mr Arthur Macshane, of no particular place in this wide world. There was also Robert King, a noted jockey and blackleg, and one Jeremiah Simpson, a linen-draper who had large acquaintance in the world of fashion and, amongst those who knew him, had the reputation of a most thorough-paced and subtle scoundrel.

Previous to the arrival of these gentry, Mr Ashworth had taken care to remove his mother from the Hall; she was gone to Ireland to spend a month or two with her relatives there. The coast being thus clear, there was no let or hindrance to the establishment of a system of bachelor housekeeping, admirably suited to the taste of the guests and their entertainer. My readers need not fear that I shall here enter into a description of the orgies of those festive weeks. I cannot describe what I never saw. But it seems traditions still exist, after the lapse of nearly forty years, of the wild, furious, and fantastic revelry which then, night after night, rung through the passages and galleries of Ashworth Hall. The astounded tenantry soon learnt what they were to expect from their profligate young landlord: he cared nothing for their welfare, thought nothing of their good opinion. All his efforts seemed to be directed to the grand end of wasting his substance in riotous living. When two months had elapsed, his guests left the Hall, and he left it with them. News soon came that he and they were gone down into the north to attend the Doncaster races at which King, the jockey, was to cut a distinguished figure. From Doncaster, they scoured up to town. King had cut a distinguished figure and was laid up in lavender for fraud of an aggravated description. His patrons left him, in trouble, without much remorse, for it was never their way to allow the mishap of one of their number to cause a halt in the headlong onward race of the rest. The whole winter was spent in town, and at last in spring, Ashworth came back to Hampshire.

He had now sown his first crop of wild oats. I say 'his first crop', for after this many another seed time came in which he scattered the grain with a lavish hand. However, he now rested awhile from this work and married. As I have said before, his bride's family name was Wharton, and she was a native of Yorkshire. It may be supposed that Ashworth's better feelings were uppermost when he selected her. She was a woman endowed with three or four good qualities: grace, sense, sweet temper, and pleasing aspect. I do not like to describe her appearance by dazzling epithets; I do not like to call her beautiful, or handsome, or fascinating. A description of a quiet character would render a more accurate idea of her form and manner. She was rather pale, and her features were soft and harmonious. Her eyes were hazel, and her hair light brown. Her air and mien were altogether ladylike, and her voice had a felicitous sweetness in its tone.

To this lady, Mr Ashworth became greatly attached. I do not mean as a lover, but as a husband. He cannot here be accused of the sin of inconstancy, for the longer he lived with her, the more dependent he seemed to grow on her society and presence. It appeared that in her he had found realized one of those dreams which young men weave, of a being lovely to their eyes and congenial to their minds, whom some spend their lives in seeking and never find.

Mrs Ashworth doubtless had faults, but they were of a kind that never annoyed her husband's fastidious taste. She was refined, gentle, and intelligent. She was also mild-tempered and kept round him a peaceful household. He could not find it in his heart, now, to break up the calm of his halls with the sacrilegious riot that had once rung along their rafters. Those who knew him in after life can hardly credit that for five years he should have kept his wandering bark anchored fast in a bay so placid, but so it was.

Some of my readers may never before have heard of Mr Ashworth and may not know the circumstances of his married life. They will doubtless conclude that his wife must have been a happy woman, living always with a husband she greatly loved and who was indisputably tender and faithful to her. It often happens that when the circumstances of a case seem perfectly clear, and it appears impossible that any juster conclusion can be drawn from them than the one which strikes us at first sight, we nevertheless find, on a closer inspection, that we were all wrong and that, as usual, outward appearances are deceitful.

Mrs Ashworth was a young and lovely woman, married to a young, handsome, and talented man. She lived in a fine old mansion with an English park around it, green and wide, with noble oaks, such as form the pride of England, crowning the slopes that were trodden by deer, with the woodlands and broad cultured fields of a southern county stretching far round. Imagine this lady walking alone in some green lane between the pastures or cornfields of her husband's estate. She has no attendant but that large Newfoundland dog, Roland, which for her sake was, in aftertimes, kept with careful attention at the Hall. Surely if you could see the face which is shaded by that straw hat, it would express happiness. She turns, startled at the sudden chirp of a bird on that hazel spray above her. Her eyes and cheek are wet with tears. So true it is that the happiest amongst us have, like the Italian lady, our dreary inner chamber, with the curtained recess shrouding some veiléd woe whose very remembrance clouds all the sunshine of our life.

Have I not said before that Mr Ashworth, in his early youth, was strange and unaccountable? Have I not hinted that he hid eccentric fantasies in his nature that seemed bordering sometimes on the frenzies of a madman? Mr Ashworth, after his marriage, changed his habits. But was it possible that he should change the temperament of his constitution or the texture of his brain? He never now writhed his limbs into the distorted and impossible attitudes of a harlequin. He never rolled his eyes or writhed his features like one stricken with epilepsy. He never started suddenly from his seat amongst his guests in his lady's drawing room and, falling almost upon her piano, let pour forth the overcharged excitement of his soul in strains of wild, musical inspiration. He never drank and cursed and fought till even a hardened villain like Daniels believed him mad, nor did he discharge firearms at random over his own dining table nor fling about shovels full of hot coals among his astounded comrades, declaring with hideous blasphemy that thus he gave them a foretaste of that hell to which they were all hastening. But, I anticipate, this was not one of the freaks of his youth; it was an exploit of his middle-age, one of his Yorkshire sprees. These things, I say, he did not do. On the contrary, his equable and high deportment was now as polished and calm as that of any gentleman in the land. But the eccentricity that was suppressed in one shape broke forth in another and that, far more peculiar and afflicting.

Mrs Ashworth, in the first three years after her marriage, had two children, boys. These were both put out to nurse in a farmhouse on the estate, where they continued till both were stout, healthy urchins capable of toddling after the poultry, cows, and horses, with the rough little rustics with whom they had been reared. Everyone then expected that they would be summoned back to the Hall and put under the guardianship of nurses, to be dressed and taught and waited on like other gentlemen's children. But no one took any notice of them. It had before been remarked that Mr Ashworth had never been known to ask after his sons or express the slightest interest in their welfare. Mrs Ashworth did, indeed, sometimes visit them, but she always came late in the evening, stayed but a little while, and often left them with tears in her eyes and a look as mournful as if she never expected to see them more.

By degrees, it began to be whispered amongst the servants and tenantry that Mr Ashworth had an antipathy to his children, and it was said he had resolved never either to own them or see them. Incredible as this rumour at first seemed, time has shown in what strange truth it was founded. And Edward and William Ashworth have since proved it well, in the neglect and hardships of their youth and the struggles and exertions of their manhood. Mr Ashworth's feelings must, I should think, have resulted from the same principle which caused the Empress Catherine's hatred of her son, Paul. Whatever was his motive, it was one which influenced him through his whole life: he never owned his sons, he never spoke to them, he never extended to them the aid of a farthing. As Mr Edward was accustomed to say, as he sat in his countinghouse in Yorkshire, thumbing over the ledger and calculating his profits for that year: let nobody talk to him of a father. He was the son of his own works. Who helped him to set up business? Who gave him a capital when he first began piece-making? He was thankful to say that he did not owe that old, broken-down scoundrel in Hampshire as much as would pay an hour's wages to one piecer in his mill.

I think I have now said enough to show that Mrs Ashworth, being as I have described her a woman of feeling and tenderness, could not be entirely happy. Much as she loved her husband, nature compelled her also to love her children and perhaps with the more painful intensity of attachment as so strange a bar was stretched between them and her and so stern a mandate issued against its removal.

When she had been married four years, she had another child. Mr Ashworth, being informed of its birth, asked if it was a son or a daughter. The nurse answered, a daughter. A kind of cloud seemed to pass from his face, and he said, 'It must remain here and be nursed at home.' When this news was brought to the mother, she looked up with an air of pleased surprise. Her countenance changed. She seemed to revive as if she thought there was an additional call for her to recover and live. More was betrayed of her past sufferings in this moment of delight for a present blessing than she had ever confessed before by complaint or tear. Mrs Ashworth was one of those people who, to the last, would have smiled at grief if the cup which contained it had been administered by the hand she loved.

The day of retribution drew near.

It is of no use delaying what I have to say or approaching it by a circuitous route. Ashworth loved his Mary as much as man ever loved woman. He had pierced her heart but knew not how deep the wound was gone. Who could think that an exterior so calm concealed mortal pains? He lived in a dream beside her, as men often do beside those they adore. But 'the time of sleep, for him, had glided by.' In his dream he had walked with an angel in the land of Beulah. He was now, like Bunyan, to awake and to find himself alone in the [undeciphered] and of a wilderness.

She died, quietly one summer evening after Mr Ashworth, at her request, had raised her in his arms from her couch to look at the sunset from the window. She turned from the shining crimson of the sky, dropped her head on his shoulder, and with a brief struggle, expired.

Mrs Ashworth was much lamented. She was one who had made few enemies in the course of her life and many friends. Her servants and acquaintance regretted her. Her children were too young to care for their loss, but her husband received a shock from the event whose severity was attested by the great change it wrought in the whole course of his subsequent life. His heart was not broken by it; his vigour was not extinguished. He loved more than once afterwards with almost insane ardour, but he

'Never found another
To free his hollow heart from pining.'

That attachment to home, which had formed a prominent feature in his character during his wife's life, died with her. The poetic tenderness of his nature, which he had ever allowed to linger round her, seemed to follow its object to the grave and to have been sealed up under the same heavy marble which sank over her remains. Who ever after her death saw tenderness in him? None, unless it might be the little bereaved child to whom Mrs Ashworth had bequeathed her name and blessing.

Misfortunes never come singly. Ashworth had known long that he was a ruined man, and, within a month after his lady's death, the whole world shared in that knowledge. I have mentioned the dissolute extravagance of his youth: that extravagance had, even before his succession to the estate, completely undermined the property he was to inherit. Hitherto he had contrived to delay that catastrophe which he knew must at last come, and he had long lived in secret misery in the prospect of destruction which must involve one dearer to him than himself. She was now removed. He at once relaxed the nerves which had been strained to avert this ruin. The avalanche slid down; all sunk under its descent. Ashworth was declared insolvent; his estate was seized by creditors, and an execution stripped the walls of Ashworth Hall. His mother, who was still living, took charge of his children. It was well she did so, for he seemed to have forgotten their existence. For himself, feeling no call to remain under the roof where 'all his household gods lay shivered round him', he left the neighbourhood and disappeared no one knew whither.

Thus I close one chapter in the life of Alexander Ashworth. It contains but three incidents, important ones all: his birth, his bridal, and his bankruptcy.

# CHAPTER II

The last sentence seems to indicate that I am writing a regular biography of this gentleman, but if my readers think so, they will find themselves mistaken. Biography is not my forte, and especially the biography of such a man. I would as soon think of sitting down and compiling a systematic life of Lord Brougham. What but an *ignis fatuus*, that carries its lantern over moor and moss through impossible places, can be expected to trace the steps of such a rover. I should be lost if I attempted to venture into the dusk wilds where I see his wandering light gleaming for a moment on the reedy pools among which it flits. No, reader, if you go with me you must keep the highroad, the railway across Chat Moss. We will talk with all whom we meet, and sometimes, at intervals, Ashworth with his light will flit across our path, perhaps pause and turn twice or thrice in his strange gyrations, then glide away, where we must never follow.

I have little to do with the fifteen years that succeeded the death of Mrs Ashworth. It seems a long space in a man's life to pass over almost in silence, and it was, besides, by far the most stirring and eventful period of Alexander's existence. But I repeat it: I cannot follow him in those strange political and commercial speculations which will hereafter give their originator a place in the historical annals of his day.

The northern counties of England were the scene of his exploits; from the time of his bankruptcy he was lost to the south. He had dived under water and reappeared far from the spot where he vanished. But it was not only his place that he had changed. His character, his aspect, his deportment seemed all to have undergone a thorough transformation. He left Ashworth in Hampshire a gentleman, aristocratic in look, language, manner, tastes, feelings, habits, prejudices. Three months had hardly elapsed when he arrived at the Strafford's Arms Inn in Wakefield, Yorkshire, dressed in a green Newmarket coat, white cords, and topboots, riding on a spirited and powerful horse and followed by a large drove of cattle. About three under-drovers were in his train, and by his side rode four gentlemen who might have been recognized, by those who had previously had the honour of their acquaintance, as Thaddeus Daniels, Esquire; George Charles Gordon, Esquire; Arthur Macshane, Esquire; and Robert King, Esquire. The last named gentleman we left twenty years ago in some trouble in Doncaster.

Thaddeus Daniels was, as I have said before, an Irish gentleman, a man vigorous in body and mind but of sullied honour, and one whose moral principles had been learnt in the school of the French Revolutionists. His wife was that Harriet whose name I mentioned as having been involved in the shade of Alexander Ashworth's early vices. Daniels knew her whole history, yet he did not scruple to marry her. But after marriage, he treated her very cruelly. She was a woman whose hapless lot seems to have been lit with few gleams of happiness. Her childhood was rendered miserable by the severity of a step-mother. When she grew up, one fatal fault destroyed her peace of mind forever. The misery of her married life drove her to frenzy. She repeated the error which had before cost her so dear, and a sad and lonely death was the atonement which an outraged conscience and broken heart exacted for the double sin.

Mr Daniels was eight years older than Mr Ashworth. It was he, in conjunction with Robert King, who had given him his first lessons in vice, lessons which had been learnt so well that now the pupil surpassed his preceptors and was ready to execute schemes which they scarcely dared plan. Daniels's hereditary fortune was gone, the same way as Ashworth's. He was therefore quite ready to join him, hand and heart, in the speculation which was to win back their alienated possessions – a daring speculation it was, embracing schemes of political charlatanerie and commercial fraud, unparalleled in any previous portion of our history.

I have said that Ashworth's father was a radical in politics. Ashworth himself, in his youth and during his married life, seemed to care for none of these things. He espoused no side but spoke with equal contempt of Whig and Tory, government and opposition. But after that event which stunned his better feelings and stirred to storm the troubled elements of his nature, he yielded to the bent of his spirit and, still despising all acknowledged powers and all existing institutions, stepped forth at once a fierce and avowed Republican. Here Daniels could warmly cooperate with him. The same continental school which had taught him his moral code gave him also his political bias: he was a disciple of Barras and Mirabeau. Many points of Irish and French character are congenial. Ferocity, treachery, and turbulence are strong characteristics of both nations. Daniels combined them all in perfection, adding the deceitful attribute of reckless animal hilarity. I have said nothing yet of Gordon and Macshane. They were scoundrels both, and penniless scoundrels, too. The variations of their character consisted in Gordon's having the most of sullen malignancy, and Macshane the least of a gentleman-like sense of honour. He too was an Irishman, and he too had had the advantage of a Gallic education. I shall give a true idea of the refinement of his moral feelings when I say that Harriet, Daniels' wife and Ashworth's mistress, was Arthur Macshane's own sister. He knew that she had been ruined by the last and brutally ill-treated by the first, yet he did not scruple to be the follower of one and the comrade of the other. Notwithstanding this, Macshane was a better man than either Daniels or Gordon. He had some generosity of heart and some warmth of feeling, qualities of which the other two were wholly innocent. What shall I say of Robert King? He was a small, mean-looking man who could not show so fine a form or strong an arm as his aristocratic companions, but who made his subtilty do the work of their strength. I seem to see that individual just now. He was low and somewhat stooped in the shoulders. He had a very bad countenance: his nose was long, rather Hebrew; his eyes, close together and small; his hair, very red. He was a man of talent in his line. Ashworth appreciated his abilities and kept him about his person for many years.

Such were the individuals Alexander Ashworth chose for his associates in his great triple character of demagogue, cow-jobber, and horse jockey. As in former times, he led. He was the Satan — they, the Beelzebub, the Belial, the Moloch, and the Mammon. Now what more need I say of the career of these heroes through the northern counties, through Lancashire, Yorkshire, Westmoreland, Cumberland, Durham, and Northumberland; of their attendance at fairs and markets; of their wholesale bargaining for oxen and horses; of their political spouting and speechifying in the streets? Is there an old grazier in Craven, a superannuated horse dealer in the East Riding, a sexagenarian farmer in any of the provinces north of the

Humber who cannot tell far better than I can of the great firm of Ashworth and Company, who cannot describe the appearance of the heads of that firm as they rode beside their great droves of cattle? Ashworth, a tall, handsome man and a most daring horseman; Daniels, heavier, darker, and broader; Gordon, sulky looking with straight black eyebrows; Macshane, a reckless chap with curled red hair and red whiskers. Many mercantile men too are living, in Leeds and Manchester and Liverpool, who can remember the market dinners given by Ashworth, the wild riot of the tables at which he presided, his own feats of drinking, his oaths, his strange, fantastic talk, his wild whims, his blasphemous and seditious after-dinner speeches. These things are not forgotten and never will be. Ashworth was a popular man in the commercial districts. The smutty, intelligent mechanics of Manchester and of the West Riding of Yorkshire adored him. He disseminated the poison of his atheistical and republican notions through their mills and combing shops, and, in those grim temples, he was set up as a god to which they willingly bowed down. Daniels was liked too; his convivial talents recommended him at all public dinners. He knew well how to disguise a traitor's heart under the features of a jovial Irish gentleman.

I have not yet touched upon Mr Ashworth's religious experience. It was during an attack of delirium tremens, the result of some weeks of reckless debauchery, that he took it into his head to preach and pray with fanatic fervour in all the towns, villages, and hamlets which lay in his route. His doctrine varied from the lowest Arminianism to the highest Calvinism. His wild frenzy and eloquence made many converts whose zeal, however, ere long cooled before the returning drunkenness and debauchery of their apostle. This fit lasted little better than a month. It recurred, however, at remote intervals in some subsequent periods of his life. Such is the brief sketch I give of the transactions comprised in that space of fifteen years – omitting only some passages of private guilt which broke up the peace of more than one family and introduced sin and sorrow to hearths where those dark guests, till then, had been strangers. Before this time, Alexander Ashworth had answered for it all at a tribunal where his high talents, far from availing to obtain him an acquittal, will only double the weight of his just condemnation.

And now the reader will begin to remember that when Mrs Ashworth died, she left behind her three children, the eldest of whom was scarcely four years old. What has become of those three? Where and what are they? Edward and William were sent by their grandmother to a public school – Harrow, I think. Had she lived, they would probably have been transferred from thence to one of the universities. Her death, however, prevented this arrangement. Edward, the eldest, pushed his way through the rough life of a schoolboy without much damage either to his feelings or his health. I never could hear that he was much liked at Harrow or that he formed any very sentimental Orestes and Pylades sort of friendships amongst his companions. Probably he had no genius for that kind of attachment. Even if the seeds of tender affection had originally existed in his nature, fate had so ordered it that they never had any chance of cultivation. He had no home, no father or mother. He had, it is true, a grandmother who seemed disposed to treat him kindly, but perhaps there was a want of sympathy between his nature and hers, for he was never observed to meet her kindness with a corresponding degree of gratitude. He might have loved his little sister but had no chance of showing his regard, as she had been separated from him from the day of her birth. However, he had a brother, an only brother, but one year younger than himself. Probably all the fond feelings of his nature were centered here. If so, it was a fondness too deep for words or even actions – for no one ever discovered its existence. Thus untroubled by puling sentiment, Edward Ashworth grew up a strong and hardy boy: well made, not too tall for his weight, with features as proportionate as his figure and a countenance whose expression was capable of various interpretations according to the humour of those who studied it. You might call it keen-spirited and self-possessed or selfish, insolent, and hardened. No one, however, could deny that it indicated active sense and ready talent, though some might fail to perceive the traces of generous feeling or chivalric honour. Edward pushed his way through the school. He sought the regard neither of masters nor schoolfellows, but both feared him. He was a dangerous lad, ever inclined to disaffection and rebellion, constantly breaking bounds and then adroitly transferring the punishment due to himself to the shoulders of some wretched fag. He had no taste for learning and never aspired after the attainments of honours.

William Ashworth differed considerably from Edward, yet he was scarcely better liked. He was quieter in manner but not more cordial in feeling. His temper was not so violent; it was cool and well controlled. He had not Edward's disposition for bullying and fighting because he was not so muscular. Once or twice, when compelled to fight with a boy stronger than himself, he submitted to a tremendous punishment with Indian doggedness and taciturnity. His forte lay rather in endurance than action. At first sight, you might have said William was an amiable boy, for he was fair and had curling light hair and a remarkably clear blue eye. But you soon discovered a want of candour, of openness, of frankness in his character. He told you nothing of his own feelings. His remarks upon those of others were cynical and sneering. Then he had a solitary turn, displeasing and unnatural in a schoolboy. In this respect, he was worse than Edward, who never shunned his companions (though when with them, he was often quarrelling and wrangling). On a holiday afternoon, William would steal off on some lonely quest of his own, and nothing awakened his slumbering, deep hate so effectually as the circumstance of being followed and watched by the other boys. If one of his favourite haunts happened to be discovered, it was remarked that he abandoned it from that time and would never return to it but wandered away in search of another and remoter place of rest. William differed from Edward in being rather fond of books – not however of his regular studies for in them he was careless and indifferent. But he sought eagerly after miscellaneous literature, and, when he had got hold of a book he liked, he would lie on his back for hours together in the shade, lost in its perusal. This, however, was a favourite position

with him when he had no book and nothing to do but look up
at the clouds and sky, visible by glimpses, through the twinkling
leaves of a tree.

William and Edward had no mutual companionship. They
had quarrelled and fought more than once, and Edward, being
the stronger, had severely thrashed William. It was his way not
always strictly to observe the rules of fair fighting. On one or
two occasions after previous provocation, when he found his
junior was in his power, after he had got the latter down, he
had struck and struck and struck again till the blood rushed out
of William's mouth and nose. This was an hereditary trait, a
legacy derived from his amiable grandfather. It was probably
treasured up with care in the memory of the young gentleman
who received it, amongst whose many brilliant good qualities, I
never heard mentioned a readiness to forgive.

When Edward was eighteen and William seventeen, their
grandmother died. She left them no fortune, for her jointure
returned to her son. Their resources ceased at once; they had
no longer the means of remaining at Harrow. Both accordingly
quitted the school with a moderate wardrobe and a small
property of one sovereign and some odd shillings each. They
found no path ready marked out for them in the world, no
profession open to their ambition, no relation willing to give
them a helping hand. The young fellows were quite alone, and
under these circumstances, they soon went down into obscurity
– dived, as their father had done, but into a worse gulf than he
had ever visited, a gulf prepared for them by their own utter
inexperience and forlornness. They shook hands with poverty.
Grinding hardship, want, famine and almost nakedness were the
gifts she gave into their bosom. We leave them thus awhile
with the darkness and vacuum of cold waves round them. The
divers may rise into daylight again, ere long, bearing in their
hands pearls, such pearls as are found in the dreary seas of
adversity.

Let us now ask after the girl. It is as if we had turned from two
plants of heath rooted on the windward side of a hill to look at
a flower carefully cultivated under a frame. And yet I might

recall that metaphor, for Miss Ashworth, like her brothers, had
never known such attention and affection as a parent can
bestow. She too had been sent early to school, but the
difference of her life there was such as exists between a public
school for young gentlemen and a private, first-rate London
establishment for young ladies. Miss Ashworth, though seldom
visited by friends, was always treated with respect both by her
governesses, the teachers, the masters, and her companions,
because the accomplishments she was taught were costly and
numerous and her appointments and dress were of the most
recherché and expensive order. Her father seldom came to see
her, but when he did come, his carriage, his fine horses, his
own very distinguished appearance never failed to make a deep
impression on the mistress of the first-rate establishment. It must
be remembered Mr Ashworth was now getting rich again. He
had purchased back Ashworth Hall and was adding to it estates
in Yorkshire. Even without these advantages, it is probable Miss
Ashworth's own mien and deportment might have secured her
a degree of consideration from those round her. I select the
word 'consideration' in preference to warmer terms, such as
'affection' or 'attachment', for the young lady had the character
of being thought somewhat proud and exclusive. It is not
impossible there might be a resemblance in her disposition to
that of her brother William. It is certain she was reserved. She
communicated no secrets; she took to herself no bosom friend.
There was one good point in her character. Though shy and
distant to the elder and more dashing of her companions, she
was usually kind to the younger and smaller fry. Her kindness
was certainly of a quiet order and seldom exhibited itself except
when they were in difficulty and distress. But if there was a hard
task to be learnt or a dreaded punishment to be averted, Miss
Ashworth was generally willing to do what she could for the
sufferer. Also, if any signs of tyranny were exhibited by the
elder ladies, her word was seldom wanting to condemn the
despotism.

Miss Ashworth had been a very troublesome pupil, very
willful and intractable when she was first brought to the school,
a little spoilt girl of six years old. But as she grew up, she

became more quiet and polished and very attentive to her studies which, indeed, offered little difficulty to her, for her capacity was good and even superior. She had especially a peculiar talent for music, probably hereditary. In this art she seemed to take a silent but deep delight, and her music master, himself a noted professor, soon pronounced her the pride of his soul. By degrees, Miss Ashworth rose to be one of the *prima donnas* of the school. Her governess also grew very proud of her, for her appearance and accomplishments did the establishment great credit. Still, though many respected Miss Ashworth, few indeed loved her. She seemed careless of the regard of most of those about her. Whether this carelessness was the result of cold-heartedness and want of feeling or whether it had another source, it shall be our business to inquire hereafter.

Miss Ashworth had now nearly completed her sixteenth year. Notice had been given that this was to be her last half-year at school. The Christmas vacation had arrived. Tomorrow all the London schools were to break up, and this was the evening of the grand examination and of the distribution of prizes. We have had enough of narrative and *didactis*: I must now come more closely to the point and endeavour to illustrate character by the occasional introduction of scenes and dialogue. I am not going to descend into the large schoolroom or the brilliantly lighted drawing room of Mrs Turner's establishment where a gay company was then assembled, and twenty young ladies elegantly dressed were showing off their accomplishments and receiving the rewards of their half-yearly exertions. The deep tone of a grand piano resounded through the whole house. There was a noise of laughter of many voices and of general gaiety below, but while this carnival reigned downstairs, silence filled the upper chambers. In one of them, a single candle was burning. Its light, though dim, showed all the signs of packing and preparation, strewed on the beds, the chairs, and the chests of drawers. Boxes of all descriptions encumbered the floor. One of those slaves called a half-boarder was kneeling in the middle of the room busily engaged in packing a large hair trunk. Gusts of rain pattered against the bedroom window giving evidence that it was a wet December night.

An hour elapsed during which the business of packing went on silently and quickly. No one appeared in the bedroom but this half-boarder, and she sometimes left it to seek for missing articles in the other chambers. Her candle then vanished with her, and all behind remained in total darkness and silence. But the scene was now going to change. Doors were heard opening below, and a burst of voices sounded through the passage. The examination was over, and the pupils set free. Steps were audible, quickly ascending the staircase; the lobby filled, and they came laughing and jumping into the bedroom. The majority of those who now entered were tall and fine-looking girls, the élite of the school, all very elegantly attired in their gala dresses. Frocks of blond and satin swept past the drudge-like half-boarder, still kneeling on the floor, presenting no very flattering contrast to her dark merino gown made high and bordered only with a narrow tucker. The ladies took no notice of this person who was not of their caste but gathered in groups by their dressing-tables which stood in the window recesses. The room was filled with talk, and in the general hum, sentences only could be snatched here and there.

'Well, I am so glad it is over! I did tremble when I had to play that sonata. Did I do it well?'

'Oh, yes, and did I repeat that scene out of Racine well? Did I speak it with a good accent?'

'Yes, excellent, but I think it was abominable of Mrs Turner not to give me the music prize. I shall tell Papa when I go home, and I don't think he will allow me to return.'

'Oh, there is such partiality. Mama says she disapproves of the school on that very account.'

'Your mama is mistaken then,' interrupted another young lady of somewhat imposing appearance. 'I think Mrs Turner has distributed the prizes very fairly.'

'Yes, she never leaves you out, Miss De Capell. You are one of her favourites.'

Miss De Capell turned away with an air of silent scorn and continued a conversation, in which she had before been engaged, with two dark-haired, Spanish-looking girls whom she addressed by the names of Julia and Harriet Daniels and who indeed were no other than the daughters of Thaddeus Daniels, Esquire. This conversation ran chiefly on what had taken place during the examination and on the dress and appearance of such as had received prizes. Mutual compliments were also interchanged.

'You did look so well, Amelia, when you went up to take the drawing prize – quite handsome.'

'Nonsense, Harriet, not half so well as you. That pink gauze dress suits your complexion so exactly. By the by, what did you think of Miss Ashworth?'

'Oh, I don't know. The same as usual – she looked proud.'

'She always does, but she is very clever. What a great many prizes she has got!'

'She and you are both to leave this half-year, I suppose, Miss De Capell?'

'Yes.'

'Will you visit with each other when you go down into Yorkshire?'

'I don't know. Perhaps the Ashworths may go to reside in Hampshire, but I must ask that half-boarder whether she has packed my things properly.'

The stately Miss De Capell walked towards the drudge and addressed her.

'Hall, have you put up my desk?'

'Yes.'

'And my workbox?'

'Yes.'

'Not my dressing case, I hope?'

'Yes, in the bottom of the trunk.'

'How very stupid of you! You might be certain I should want it. You will just please to get it out again.'

'I shall have to unpack the whole box, and it is corded,' said the half-boarder.

'I cannot help that,' was the haughty reply. 'I must have my dressing case.'

The drudge paused from her work. She answered still looking down.

'I think that unreasonable, Miss De Capell. I have so much to do.'

'It is your duty, I suppose, to wait upon us,' retorted the other, evidently a spoilt child of wealth. 'You will be kind enough to oblige me, or I shall find it necessary to complain to Mrs Turner.'

The half-boarder did as she was bid and with hurried fingers proceeded to unknot the hard rough cords she had had such difficulty in fastening.

Amelia De Capell returned to her companions.

'Oh,' said she, clasping her hands as if a sudden ecstasy had come over her feelings, sweeping away every recollection of Hall, the drudge, 'Oh, how delightful it will be tomorrow when the carriage, our own carriage, drives up to the door, and Papa alights from it, and Nicholson rings the bell and thunders at the knocker. Then, when I have bid you all good-bye and am fairly settled in the barouche, close at Papa's side, and when we dash off – farewell to Kensington, and hey for canny Yorkshire and sweet De Capell Hall!'

Miss Amelia was a handsome, blooming girl, and she looked beautiful, as her eyes sparkled with the anticipation of pleasure. Few indeed could look out on a brighter prospect than what lay before her. She was an only daughter and destined to be a wealthy heiress. Her father, notwithstanding his aristocratic name, was a man in business – a merchant – but one of those merchants who resemble princes. His style of living, his house, his carriage, his horses, and servants might rival a nobleman's. My readers must not suppose from the little scene I have just described that Miss Amelia was a very ill-natured or unpleasant young lady. On the contrary, she was very much liked amongst those she considered her equals, for with such she made herself very agreeable. Her mother was a proud and senseless woman, and she had been taught from early childhood that inferiors were persons to be kept at a distance and treated haughtily. The indulgence and flattery of a large circle of rich relations had taught her to consider herself something unparalleled. Under these circumstances, it was only her natural good humour, her beauty, and a certain portion of sense which prevented her from becoming something insufferable. Miss De Capell and Miss Ashworth had never agreed well together. Their mutual pride had kept them at a distance. But Miss Ashworth was free from some of Miss De Capell's faults. She had never been spoilt by the idiotic flattery of relations. Then, her mind was decidedly of a higher order, and her tone of feeling very different. She had the habit of thinking by herself, of pondering over the puzzles of human nature. She was more original and infinitely less conceited. To speak truth, I cannot well tell what she was, but I will bring her onto the stage and let her speak for herself.

The bedroom was again deserted for a bell had rung below, summoning all the school to supper. Even the half-boarder had rested a moment from her endless packing, and, though she was not gone down with the rest, her glass of milk and plate of bread had been brought to her, and she was seated on one of the boxes, eating her meal slowly and thoughtfully. A young lady also had remained behind. She occupied a place at the foot of one of the white curtained beds, and her head was bent over a brilliantly bound volume, one of her prizes, whose plates she seemed to be examining. She shut it and rose up.

'Miss Hall,' said she, 'have you packed my trunks?'

'Yes.'

'Perhaps you cannot make room for these books? If the boxes are corded, they may be put in the pockets of the carriage.'

'I can make room easily,' said Miss Hall in a cheerful tone, and she rose with alacrity and, opening a large portmanteau, proceeded to stow away the glittering prizes.

The young lady stood by her side and watched the process. In this position the light of the single candle shone full on her, and my readers may now take a view of Miss Ashworth.

She was a form favoured by nature, not tall but well-grown and graceful. Her face was little less than beautiful, for the features were Grecian in their cast and the complexion such as suited those features, not blooming but fair and clear. She had brown hair, very simply arranged, and hazel eyes, well-opened, large and bright. Her countenance expressed full as much seriousness as vivacity.

'Where do you intend to spend the holidays, Miss Hall?' she asked, after having watched in silence till her trunk was again closed up.

'I always spend them here in London,' replied the half-boarder.

'Probably you have no parents, then?'

'No, ma'am.'

'But you have sisters or brothers?'

'I have one brother who is a surgeon on board an East India vessel.'

'Older than you, of course.'

'Yes, he is three and twenty; I am only fifteen.'

'Have you any other relations?'

'I believe I have an uncle and aunt somewhere in England, but they are rich people and of course think little about me.' The last part of the sentence was said not sadly but rather in a cheerful, matter-of-fact way and, with a glance upwards at Miss Ashworth, accompanied by a smile. It was the first time the half-boarder had looked up, and it was now seen that she had a face of a not unpleasant cast, though somewhat thin and care-worn for her age. Miss Ashworth returned the smile. In a gentle tone, she continued the conversation.

'Where did you live before you came to Mrs Turner's, Miss Hall?'

'I lived a considerable distance from London, on the borders of Lancashire,' was the reply, and the speaker again bent busily over her boxes.

'Do you feel particularly unhappy here?' again inquired Miss Ashworth.

'Oh, no ma'am, good times and bad times and all times get over. I shall be sorry, however, Miss Ashworth, when you are gone.'

'Why? I do not think I have been in the habit of speaking to you a dozen times in the course of a half-year.'

'So much the better. I wish all the young ladies had followed your example. Some of them speak to me far too often.'

'Does the insolence of that Miss De Capell and others of her class annoy you much?'

'Never for above ten minutes together.'

'Yet I have seen you cry.'

'Did you watch me, Miss Ashworth?'

'Occasionally.'

The half-boarder looked up again with an air of surprise and incredulity.

'I was not aware you ever wasted a thought about me,' said she.

'You are almost old enough to leave Mrs Turner's,' continued Miss Ashworth, after a pause.

'I am to leave her, when Mrs Turner can get me a situation as companion or nursery-governess.'

'Nursery-governess! You might do better than that!'

'Mrs Turner says I have not capacity for anything higher.'

'On what grounds does she rest that opinion?'

'You know I never say the lessons correctly that she gives me.'

'In the name of common sense, how can she expect it when the moment she has given you the pages of history to study or three pages of French prose to learn by heart, she sends you into the laundry to clearstarch a basketful of lace and muslin?'

'You notice more than I thought,' said the half-boarder, smiling again.

'Notice, Miss Hall! Do you suppose I keep my eyes shut? My only wonder is that you learn what you do. Of all the slaves of industry, you are the most indefatigable.'

'I get up early in the morning.'

'And you go to bed late at night. I have heard you stealing upstairs to your closet, long after twelve o'clock.'

'Are you awake at that time, Miss Ashworth?'

Miss Ashworth did not answer. She moved away to her own bedside and began slowly to undress. Half an hour passed in silence. Miss Ashworth had laid her head on her pillow and seemed to be asleep. The half-boarder, having finished what she had to do in this room, took her candle and was stepping on tip-toe out of the apartment.

'Ellen! Ellen Hall,' said Miss Ashworth, raising her head. 'Your name is Ellen, I think, is it not?'

'Yes.'

'Will you reach me my handkerchief out of that little top drawer?'

Miss Hall opened the drawer in question. She seemed surprised to find that it contained several volumes.

'I thought,' said she, as she handed the required handkerchief, 'that I had cleared out this chest this morning, and here is a drawer full of books. Some of Scott's, some of Byron's. I wish I had time to read them.'

'You will probably have time in the holidays,' remarked Miss Ashworth.

'Yes, but then they will not be here.'

'Look at the title page of that one you have in your hand.'

Miss Hall obeyed. A few words were written on the blank leaf: 'Mary Ashworth begs Ellen Hall to accept the accompanying volumes of Scott's and Byron's works as a farewell token of her regard.' Miss Hall dropped the book, shut the drawer and went quickly out of the room. She only got, however, as far as the threshold. There she checked herself and returned.

'I am much obliged to you,' said she approaching Miss Ashworth's bedside.

'You are quite welcome, Ellen. Good-night.' Miss Ashworth offered her hand which, as she held it out, was seen to be most beautiful and delicate. The humble dependent took it, pressed it, and, in the warmth of her gratitude, she even ventured to bend down and kiss the cheek of the proud young lady. Miss Ashworth smiled and did not repulse her. The rushing of steps upstairs broke up the scene. Miss Ashworth hastily withdrew her hand, dropped her head on the pillow, and feigned to be asleep. Miss Hall hurried away.

## CHAPTER III

As the wheel of fortune turns, her lottery throws up now a prize and now a blank. Mr Ashworth had got a grievous blank sixteen years ago when he lost his house and lands, but now again a prize seemed to have fallen to his lot. He had dissolved partnership with Daniels, Gordon, Macshane and Company. The cattle dealing business was given up, but not before it had enriched the chief originator to an extent which he himself probably had not at first ventured to hope. I do not stop to enquire whether all this mass of wealth had been fairly gained – most likely not, for Ashworth was an unscrupulous man who made a jest of such trifles as conscience and faith. But gold is gold, whether won with honour or exacted by fraud, and, if it does not purchase a man a place in heaven, a rest in Abraham's bosom, it can procure him at least a splendid mansion on earth with the daily luxury and purple clothing of Dives.

Though the house in Hampshire was again become Mr Ashworth's property, he would no more make it his home, influenced perhaps by a disinclination to revisit scenes which must necessarily recall times and events he wished entirely to forget. He now purchased, therefore, a place in Yorkshire called Gillwood, a house whose fine grounds and old woods seemed to give their owner a sort of importance in the county. He furnished the large, oak-lined rooms of this mansion in a style of splendour which would have suited well with a coronet and title and, when all was prepared, brought down his daughter to be the finishing ornament.

Could Mr Ashworth enjoy his returning good fortune? I think not. No man can run the mad career he had run so long without being jaded at the termination of his race. Mr Ashworth was a changed man. His constitution was broken up; his bodily strength, exhausted. Few could recognize the athletic drover who rode, drank, and fought so unweariedly in that tall, pale valetudinarian whose bald brow, from which the thick auburn curls had fallen quite away, looked so charged with melancholy as he roamed through the gloom of Gillwood.

Many of Ashworth's passions were dead, but ambition was not among the number. It lingered still like one live coal among surrounding ashes. Of course his ambition was of a political order, and it aspired to a seat in Parliament. His new residence was in the neighbourhood of a borough which sent two

representatives to the House. Ashworth watched for the first
vacancy, to step forward as a candidate.

As Gillwood lay in an agricultural district, indeed, in the fine
campaign country surrounding York, there were not wanting
many seats within a moderate distance whose proprietors took
an equal station with Mr Ashworth. The turreted roof of one
mansion was visible from an elevated point in Gillwood
grounds. It was seen from between the divided stems of two tall
beech trees, crowning a long upward slope of lawn. On a
summer evening, it formed a pretty object, rising grey above its
dusk woods and with a low hill of clear but faint azure far away
in the background. These grey turrets bore the name of Ripley
Towers and were the local habitation of old General West.
General West was a truculent Tory, also a veteran who had
seen service in the Indian Wars and gained a name in despatches
for his conduct on the field 'of red Assaye'.

General West and Mr Ashworth had met each other at public
dinners and once at a county meeting, held on the subject
either of corn, Catholics, or currency. On this last occasion, Mr
Ashworth had delivered a long speech, breathing of burning
patriotism and high love of freedom from beginning to end, and
when he sat down General West had established himself upon
his legs and, in a gruff voice, had characterized the whole
effusion as absolute humbug, and then, addressing the people,
had recommended them to think twice before they allowed
their judgements to be biased by sophistry of that description. It
was remarked that Mr Ashworth had been in no way stirred to
wrath by this unceremonious condemnation of his eloquent
harangue. On the contrary, he had regarded the speaker with a
look of curious and quiet scrutiny and, when he sat down, had
smiled with an expression that seemed to say, 'That old boy
knows the difference between a hawk and a handsaw.' In this
opinion he was probably not far wrong, at least so the sagacious
glance of the grey old rajah seemed to attest.

These were the only opportunities the two country
gentlemen had had of forming an acquaintance. Except indeed,
that as both were magistrates, they sometimes sat on the same
bench, when they bowed and spoke to each other civilly but

made no advances to private intimacy. In spite of this distant demeanour, an observant spectator would have said that a sort of tacit understanding existed between them, that each knew and appreciated the other's character. The mutual bow at meeting and parting was often accompanied by a furtive smile – unless in the meantime they had quarrelled, which was not unfrequently the case.

But though General West maintained no familiar communication with Mr Ashworth, it was said that this was not the case with all the inmates of Ripley Towers. A man may command armies to admiration and yet find his power ineffectual to control the members of his own family. The General was not troubled with a very large private circle. He had just one olive branch, one arrow in his quiver and that an ill-feathered one which never shot straight. In other words, he was cursed with a son who ought to have been called Absalom Rehoboam West, a sort of runagate whom his father frequently permitted to continue in scarceness. This gentleman had, by the blessing of God and the forbearance of many tutors, prolonged his days until he attained the years and stature of a man. His father had, during his boyhood and his university experience, held him in with a tight curb. But now that he had come home finished from Oxford, he slackened the reins, flung him large rope, and let him swing loose on the world. Had the old rajah, on the contrary, pulled the halter a little tighter and lifted him up high and dry over the gallows tree, the world would have been no worse for the mistake.

Absalom Rehoboam, I have said, ought to have been the name of this person, but at the baptismal font his sponsors gave him the cognomen of Arthur Ripley, and, between this Arthur and the lord of Gillwood, rumour hinted the existence of a closer social league than the General was at all aware of. It might be that the General knew it perfectly but did not care and would not meddle. He was a sly, calculating old Cossack. In this last opinion, I am strengthened by the fact that when, as it sometimes happened, friends interfered and expostulated with the General on the subject, he always suddenly became very dull of comprehension and would understand no hints and hear no advice. There was one gentleman especially, a person of a serious and severe tenue, who, being an old friend of the family and indeed godfather to Arthur himself, thought he had a right to put in a word on the subject. The person I allude to was no other than Mr De Capell, for De Capell Hall stood in the immediate neighbourhood of Gillwood and Ripley Towers.

Now Mr De Capell was, as I have said, a merchant and a man of business, but he was not the less an aristocrat. His family was as good as any in Yorkshire. But he had been a younger son and had derived no inheritance from his father's house, but a name and a certain station in society. Under these very ordinary circumstances, he had taken the very extraordinary resolution to set aside dignity, take interest as his guide, launch into trade, and seek that fortune amongst mills and warehouses, wood and oil which he was sure not to find amongst crests and coats of arms, old scutcheons and tarnished shields. Mr De Capell was well-fitted to make his way in the path he had chosen. He was a persevering, sagacious, grasping, obstinate man. His hand was closed and his heart, not too susceptible. But he had his own notions of honour and integrity, and, though he had stepped aside to dig for lucre in the company of grovelling plebians, and had been as grovelling in the pursuit of that precious ore as the lowest of them, he still retained a hidden fund of family pride that might have suited a lord. And now after a long life spent in the countinghouse, having gained immense wealth, having withdrawn his capital from trade and vested it in land, he sat down to enjoy in state what he had gained in toil.

Mr De Capell had two sons besides the daughter I have already introduced to my readers. His conduct towards these sons was rigid and harsh. He seemed fearful lest they should further tarnish the name he had himself perilled by mingling it with the pollutions of trade. John, the oldest, grew up a credit to the discipline his youth had received. He seemed a proud, correct young man, gifted with a power of perfect self-command. But little was known of him in this neighbourhood, for since his departure from college, he had resided chiefly in London, where he was said to be engaged in studying the law. Thornton, the younger, was not at all better than he should be, a thorn in his father's side, a mere scamp whom the old gentleman was on the point of disowning and disinheriting every day of his life. Amelia De Capell I have spoken of before, but I fear I gave my readers too unfavourable an impression of her character. She had her good points. She was lively, clever, and very affectionate to those she thought it no degradation to love. While I spoke of her before, I was comparing her in my heart with a mind of another order: one that could see farther, feel deeper, look higher; one whose nature was not all known at once, which you could dash off in a single sketch as satirical, lively, clever, proud, but a subject of protracted interest that might give you employment for many months before you learnt to read its indications correctly. I don't know whether the mind I allude to was better than Amelia De Capell's, but it was one liable to more varied and profound impressions, perhaps also to more numerous and rooted defects.

When old De Capell had been specially annoyed by his prodigal son, Thornton, he used to take a walk over of an evening to Ripley Towers for the purpose of condoling with the similarly afflicted master of that mansion. And now, reader, before giving you a slight sketch of one of their dolorous dialogues, I ought to premise that Mr De Capell had in his speech a slight touch of that doric called broad Yorkshire. Do not, reader, be surprised at this because, in the first place, such things were amongst even the upper classes of the Yorkshire gentry thirty years ago and, in the second place, Mr De Capell had not always exclusively associated with the upper classes but had much to do with the manufacturers of Leeds and the clothiers of Bradford.

Mr De Capell had also a habit of smoking a pipe, which he preferred to a cigar, and was fond of a small glass of brandy and water, both which luxuries he had been used to on a market day and had also occasionally partaken of in his private countinghouse. Now Mr De Capell had almost ceased to indulge in these enjoyments at home. He had an idea that they compromised his dignity. But whenever he came to see the General and they two were alone, the brandy and water and the cherry stalk were always provided, though time after time Mr

De Capell used carelessly to remark that 'there was no occasion, none at all.'

'I see no end to this wark,' remarked Mr De Capell, raising his bent body with a deep sigh as he took the pipe from his lips. He fixed his eyes on a window which was opposite to him and looked out on a snow shower then whitening the park, for it was winter. Mr De Capell did not allude to the snow, though any uninitiated listener might have fancied he did. 'They've been together again,' he continued, sighing more heavily, 'and they just corrupt one another.'

'This will be a right January night,' responded General West.

'I'm fair stalled on it. Yond' lad will bank me afore he's done.'

'It is setting in for a regular long frost, I believe.'

'I've tried every means I can think of to reform him, and I think I shall have fairly to give it up. He's a reprobate. I sometimes think it's a kind of striving against Providence to keep tewing with such a one. Last night he was treating all the raff in the country at the Ripley Arms. Your own inn, General! I can tell you, you'd only be doing justice if you took the landlord's licence from him.'

'I'll see about it.'

'And I – you'll keep seeing about it till both my lad and yours have got their necks into a halter. Did you hear how they went on when they were off on the moors together a month syne?'

'No.'

'They had two public houses open and such drinking and dancing and a ball for all the hussies and scoundrels about Pendle – I've written to John about that business. If it wor not for our John and our Amelia, I think I might lie down and dee.'

'Amelia is come home, I suppose.'

'Yes.'

'I hear she is a very fine girl. She will be a catch; you must look after her.'

'That I shall most certainly do, sir. I'll have no needy rakes marrying into my family. I did think once many a year syne that Ripley West might have done worse than taken our Amelia, if it had pleased Providence to fix it so. She'll have brass, General.

I can give her thirty thousand pounds and more than that if Thornton does not heed what he is about.'

'Yes, it would be a reasonable arrangement,' remarked the General, 'but which of these lads will hear reason? Ripley is a great swaggering Turk who, I daresay, has no particular intention of marrying for twenty years to come.'

'It would be better for himself if he should. Though I hear queer tales about him; he's varry unsteady, General.'

'He is. I agree with you.'

'And wouldn't a wife settle him a bit, think you?'

'Wouldn't he settle her? I can tell you, De Capell, Arthur Ripley would make a very bad husband if he married now.'

'You want him to sow his wild oats, then?'

'I do,' replied the worldy-wise General West. 'That was the reason I sent him to the continent last year.'

'You've strange ways of managing with your lad,' said Mr De Capell. 'I allus wished to keep mine out of temptation; you thrust yours in. "Lead us not into temptation," – is not that a part of the Lord's Prayer?'

The General laughed. 'Arthur must put up that petition for himself,' said he. 'All I mean to say is there's no use in putting guards and limitations about such a fellow as he is. Look at him and then talk of protecting him from temptation. If he were a young lady, I grant you, the case might be different. I would not have you to send your Amelia to London or Paris or Florence, unattended, to run the gauntlet of theatres, operas, cafés, etc. I would not even permit her to hear of such scenes as those I have alluded to. I would look after her in theory as well as practice. But Ripley must see the world for himself, look it boldly in the face. If he has any true ore in him, it will stand the ordeal. If he is all dross, he must perish.'

'I'm afraid he has a good bit of dross, at all events,' remarked Mr De Capell. 'He's shown naught else yet. And whatever you may say, General, I know there is an old book that tells me "evil communications corrupt good manners."'

'How is it, then, that your John has not been corrupted? At one time, he was quite as much a crony of that scamp Ripley's as Thornie is now. Yet he is a very good fellow, an admirable fellow.'

'Ay, blessings on him, he is a good lad. He's all I have to tak to – I set a deal o' store on him. If aught were to happen to him, I know not how I mught stand it,' and Mr De Capell drew out his pocket handkerchief and put it to his eyes. He had had three glasses of brandy and water.

'Come, cheer up,' said the General, 'John is well enough, I daresay. Are you aware whether he and Ripley correspond now?'

'Nay, I think Ripley has cut him almost. He's ta'en up entirely wi' that nought Ashworth. I'll tell you what, General. If I was you and had a son such as you' Arthur Ripley and he war to begin trafficking with a villain like Ashworth, a cheating, bankrupt horse dealer; a seditious, bloody Republican; a blasphemous infidel, Tom Painite, I think I would just get my will and draw a scrawk ower his name and leave ivry halfpenny I had to build a 'firmry with or to make a new dock at Liverpool. I think,' pursued Mr De Capell, taking a fresh breath and warming as he spoke, 'I think that Ashworth has earned a gibbet five times ower. Of all the robbers, of all the rascals that ever stepped, he caps the globe! Impident swindler, he should have been working in chains at Botany Bay twenty years syne. When I heard he'd bought Gillwood and had getten hisseln made a magistrate and war coming to live here, I thought I mught never have done no more good. Then t'scandal that has been talked ower him – there's Daniels' wife and there's Thurston's wife and that hussey Miss Allan and twenty more beside. And they say, General, they say that next election he's going to set up as candidate for Littlebro'. What do you think of that!' Mr De Capell struck his fist on the table as if he had clenched the case. The tumblers and decanter responded with a rattle, but the General said nothing. He only looked in a quizzical kind of way at his companion. In fact, he was a hard man of the world whom no detail of atrocities could move.

'I suppose,' observed the General after a pause. 'Ashworth has two sons somewhere whom he does not choose to own.'

'Sons born in wedlock or illegitimate children?' asked Mr De Capell.

'No, sons lawfully born and by this time grown up, I

understand. They were both at Harrow with Ripley. The eldest is now about his age – twenty.'

'And where are they?'

'The devil knows. They have not been heard of for three or four years.'

'And their father cares nought about them?'

'He does not own them.'

'He's an unnatural brute. Then, he has another child – a lass.'

'Yes, she was at school with your daughter. Does Miss De Capell ever speak of her?'

'Ay, Amelia says she was a little, proud, queer-tempered thing. But I think I must be going now for it will be a wild night.'

And so Mr De Capell knocked the ashes out of his pipe, rang for his horse and departed.

## CHAPTER IV

Miss Ashworth and Miss De Capell, being both now settled in Yorkshire, exchanged one or two formal visits, such as etiquette rendered almost indispensable as the young ladies had been school-fellows together for a period of nearly ten years. It was one fine frosty morning in January when Miss Ashworth rode over on horseback to De Capell Hall for the purpose of returning a previous visit of Miss De Capell's. She was shown into a pretty little drawing room, not like the dim antique apartments of Gillwood, but light, elegant and cheerful, for De Capell Hall was a modern house, erected by its present proprietor, and, in the freshness of its external appearance and the gilded brilliancy of its internal decorations, differed widely from the Elizabethan pile, all time-stained without and darkly panelled within.

Amelia De Capell sat by a bright fire, leaning back in one of those easy drawing room chairs invented by luxury to lounge in. A kind of embroidery frame stood by her, and various gay shades of worsteds lay on a little worktable near. These preparations for industry were, however, only for show apparently, for Miss Amelia was not working; she was reading, and the volume she held in her hand looked singularly like a novel. Miss De Capell had a companion. A very small figure sat on the opposite side of the hearth on a low stool, bending diligently over sundry silken materials with which her lap was filled. She sat quietly and seemed absorbed in her work. A little spaniel lay curled at her feet.

Miss De Capell rose to welcome her visitor. 'I am most happy to see you, Miss Ashworth, pray sit down. What a lovely morning for January.'

'Yes, but cold,' said Miss Ashworth, advancing to the fire.

'Did you come by Ripley Towers? Have you called there yet?'

'No.'

'Oh, I forgot. I daresay General West does not visit with your papa. Will you throw off your beaver?'

Miss Ashworth removed her beaver and laid it on a couch where she also placed herself, after she had duly warmed her hands which were somewhat numbed with the cold ride.

'Well,' continued Miss De Capell, who now looked very good humoured and more cordial and affable than her somewhat nonchalante guest, 'well, how do you think you shall like Gillwood? Don't you think you shall find it rather dull in winter?'

'Very,' was the reply, and you could not tell from the tone in which it was uttered whether the speaker spoke sincerely or in irony. 'Such a dark house,' she continued after a pause, 'such gloomy rooms, and Papa must needs have all the family pictures brought down from Hampshire to fill the gallery with ghosts.'

'Ah, I thought you would not like it,' continued Miss De Capell. 'Such a place, you know, is well enough to visit by way of show, very romantic and impressive, but really to pass one's life there would be too dreary. My brother John now admires the place. He is such a grave old bachelor. You shall see him, Miss Ashworth, when he comes down from London. I think he would suit you for, as far as I recollect, you are not too guilty of the sin of giddiness.'

Miss Ashworth made no remark. She was engaged in trying to attract the attention of the little spaniel on the rug by putting out her foot and withdrawing it, and, at the same time, she was furtively examining the person at whose feet the spaniel lay. Miss Ashworth's eyes had a peculiar expression when their large orbs, alive with discernment, were thus secretly directed on any particular individual.

'Go to that lady, Flora,' said a low voice, and the stranger stooped and, with a very small hand, pushed her little dog towards Miss Ashworth.

'Oh! I had forgotten to introduce to you my cousin, Marian,' exclaimed Miss De Capell. 'I beg pardon, but she is so tiny, it is easy to overlook her. Marian, this is Miss Ashworth of Gillwood. You have heard me mention her before.' The mistress of the spaniel for the first time raised her head from her work, bowed, gave one glance at the visitor, and then again her eyes fell. She seemed diffident and what the French call *craintive*. At first sight, you would have taken her for a little girl, she was so small and slightly formed. But when she looked up, her face was not that of a child. It had the expression of seventeen years. The complexion was delicate and the features also. There was something agreeable in her eyes which were blue and soft, but too often downcast. Her hair was of a pretty shade of auburn. It parted in a cluster of long curls on each side of her face and shaded her fair neck very sweetly.

'Flora does not like to leave you, I think, Miss Marian,' said the visitor. 'She is a pet, I daresay.'

'I spoil her,' replied the same quiet voice that had spoken before.

'Have you been here some time?' resumed Miss Ashworth.

'Since Amelia came home from London.'

'Then why did you not come with your cousin when she called at Gillwood?'

'Ah, that is right, Miss Ashworth,' interrupted Amelia De Capell, 'put her to the question. She is such a shy being. I cannot tell how to cure her of that foolish diffidence. She would not go with me because she said you did not know her, and she was sure you would not want her.'

'I know her now, then,' returned Miss Ashworth, 'and I hope she will not decline to accompany you when you call again.'

'Thank you,' said Marian, again venturing to raise her eyes, and she seemed to have screwed up her courage to proceed and say something more when unfortunately the rising spirit of conversation was effectually dashed by a sudden quick rap at the drawing room door and the immediate entrance of the person who had given it before Miss De Capell had time to say, 'Come in.'

'Where is Wilson, Miss Amelia?' asked someone, advancing into the room.

'In the stables or the dog kennel, no doubt. But now, sir, what do you want with him this morning?'

'What do I want? Only to say two or three words to him. But my business will keep cool, and in the meantime I will sit half an hour with you.'

Miss De Capell, with something of a flutter in her manner, resumed the chair from which she had risen, and she was followed to her seat by a towering form of slender build, a man in height though as yet only a youth in breadth. It was Mr Arthur Ripley West. We may as well introduce him at once without further parade and also announce that he is going to be our hero, for if we did not reveal this secret, the reader would soon find out.

Such an individual as this said Mr Arthur could by no means enter a drawing room occupied by three young ladies without creating a sensation. His face and form were those of a very young man, not more than one and twenty, and also a man likely to find drawing rooms scenes of easy triumph. His rich curled hair told that he was a coxcomb. His features were regular and Roman, and, in his dark smiling eyes and round his lips, there was all that expression of mingled keenness and sweetness which, since the world began, has ever been the attribute of clever, handsome scamps, of fellows who with smiles and jests can buy themselves the privilege of sinning on a grander scale than their contemporaries, of men who with genius and poetry of character can so disguise their evil deeds that a careless eye may easily mistake them for virtues, of gentlemen whom nature has gifted with haughty gallantry that they may defy to the teeth all who would stop them in the career of crime.

Mr West sat down. He had chosen his seat on Miss De Capell's right hand and leaned his head a little towards her. According to the fitness of things, he had chosen well. Miss De Capell's fine dashing appearance harmonized with his own. She made a better companion picture for him than Miss Ashworth or the diminutive Miss Fairburne could have done. And did Mr West's inclinations turn towards his companion picture, the tall, dark-haired and noble Amelia? It appeared so, for when he began to speak, he addressed his conversation to her.

'Was Wilson late home last night?'

'Late, Mr Ripley! You know as well as I do. You will ruin Wilson; indeed, you will!'

'What? Do you join the ranks of my accusers? "Et tu Brute?" I thought you always took my part. I depended on you for my defender when Papa and Mama and John and the whole tribe of the righteous rose up against me.'

'Did I accuse him, Marian?' asked Miss De Capell, appealing to her cousin. 'Did I throw the blame on him last night when Papa was so angry?'

'No,' said Miss Fairburne, stooping down to extricate the silken threads of her netting from her spaniel's paws who had got hold of them and twisted them into strange entanglement. The dog drew away the whole concern to the other end of the rug and took refuge at Mr West's feet.

'Flora, Flora!' said Miss Fairburne, 'come back.' She would not follow him to his stronghold.

'You had better come forward, I think,' said Mr West, 'or the purse will be gone past redemption.'

Miss Fairburne, however, sat still and still called, 'Flora, Flora!'

'I think you are not too civil,' remarked Amelia, stooping down to do what it appeared Mr Arthur might as well have done. She rescued the purse and returned it to its owner. 'You ought to take a few lessons in the science of *petits soins*, I think, Mr Ripley,' she continued. 'I should have thought your travels on the continent and your six months residence in Paris might have taught you the elements of politeness, at least.'

'It has taught me some pretty sentimental ways, Miss Amelia, admiration for flowers, for instance. Do you see this snowdrop in my buttonhole?'

'Oh, yes, the first I have seen this year. How white and beautiful!' All the ladies looked at it. Even Miss Fairburne raised her head and hazarded one glance.

'That snowdrop is ladylike,' continued Mr West. 'It was growing in a nook of moss at a tree root. Probably I may write a sonnet on it sometime.'

'You will show it to us when it is written?' said Miss De Capell.

'Oh, yes, it shall be fairly copied out in a satin-bound album, and I will bring it and deposit it in your lap. Miss Fairburne?' She was again obliged to raise her head, for he paused till her lifted eyes showed she had given him her attention.

'Where is your drawing, the sketch of the bridge?'

'In my portfolio, but I think it is not quite finished.'

'Allow me to see it.'

Miss Fairburne got up. She opened the portfolio which lay on a side table and was searching amongst its multifarious contents. As she turned over the paintings and engravings, another hand aided her in the search. She hastily looked up; Mr West stood close behind her. He was stooping over her shoulder. She did not stir. Her fingers continued mechanically to stray amongst the squares of cardboard and sheets of tissue paper.

'That is the bridge,' said Mr West. 'You have got it now.'

'Have I?' returned Marian, and then she coloured, confused and vexed at her own absence of mind. She gave him the picture, and, as he took it from her hand, his eye looking down met hers glancing up. I have said Mr West's eyes were dark and smiling. They were also singularly piercing. It was not easy to meet their gaze steadily.

'This is a pretty little sketch,' said he, after looking at it for a few minutes in silence. 'But the arch is not quite straight.'

'I always fail there,' murmured Miss Marian.

'Get your pencil, and we will alter it,' said the connoisseur.

She quickly obeyed him. He took a seat by the table, and, while he applied some finishing and corrective touches, Miss Fairburne stood and watched. Her head now reached the altitude of his. When both were standing, it was a fairy by a monument, the tall bully of London.

'Now will it do, Marian?' said he. His words and manner were quite simple, and yet Miss Fairburne looked almost agitated.

'It is much better,' she replied.

It was indeed. A few dark and bold dashes had changed it from a feeble, flimsy, though rather pretty and delicate thing to an artistical looking sketch. Mr West replaced it in the portfolio.

'Will you paint my snowdrop, Marian?'

'If you wish me, but it will fade before I finish it.'

'I hope not.'

'It is faded now.'

'No,' said Mr West, 'as I see it, it is not. Let me point it out to you.' He directed a sort of side-glance towards the hearth. The two ladies seated there had their backs towards him. They were likewise now conversing together and seemed not to be listening to him.

'Come here,' said he in an undertone. He took Miss Fairburne's hand and turning her towards a psyche mirror, pointed to the reflection of a delicate fairy form which she could not deny to be her own. 'That is my snowdrop,' said Arthur Ripley. At this announcement, Miss Fairburne did not seem to be so much embarrassed as she had been before. Nervous people often appear more composed at a crisis than when the cause of embarrassment is slight.

'No, no,' said she, venturing to look right in his face, 'you are jesting. I see you think me silly because I am not so self-possessed and accomplished as Amelia. I cannot help being shy and awkward, but I quite understand your character, Mr West.'

'Do you? What is it?'

'You are rather satirical, and, when you see me so foolish and bashful, you often feel tempted to amuse yourself at my expense. But I wish you would promise not to do so again, for it is the very thing that makes me so uncomfortable.'

I know not whether Mr West would have given the required promise, but just then Miss Ashworth rose to take her leave. She looked no ordinary figure as she stood up in her purple riding habit and, having put on the beaver she had removed, threw back the veil from her statue-like and beautiful features. She gave her hand to Miss De Capell and Miss Fairburne and hardly bent her head to Mr West. She was not of tall stature; she scarcely indeed reached the middle height. Yet there was something of the princess about her as she passed from the apartment. Three minutes after, she cantered past the window on her beautiful pony, followed by a groom on horseback.

'Proud as Lucifer!' ejaculated Miss De Capell.

'Who is she, in the name of Juno?' asked Mr West.

'Miss Ashworth, only daughter and heiress of Alexander Ashworth, Esquire, of Gillwood.'

'God bless me!' replied Mr West briefly. He stood silent at the window a minute as if he were thinking, then he turned round. Shortly after this, he took his leave. 'Good morning, Miss Amelia,' said he, holding out his hand. 'Good morning, Miss Fairburne.' The words of his parting salutation were precisely the same to both ladies, but the tone and the look accompanying them were very different.

It seems then Mr West preferred his contrast rather than his likeness. When he was gone, a dead silence fell upon the drawing room. Miss De Capell sat before her embroidery frame and worked. Miss Fairburne occupied a window seat and seemed to read. Ere long the book fell on her lap. She leaned her head on her hand and sat idle. It was what she was in the habit of doing after Mr West's morning calls.

# THE MOORES

## CHAPTER 1

'Now, Sarah Julia, how do you like Aspen Place?'

'Oh, it is all very well.'

'Very well? I think it is. I flatter myself I have done the thing handsomely. Neither father-in-law nor mother-in-law can deny that I have made a liberal outlay. Here you are settled like a queen.'

'Well, Mr Moore, you promised.'

'Settled like a queen. A grand mansion, quite, one may say, in the country; an establishment of servants all smart and well drilled; capital furniture, all new – yes, there's not a stool in this house, nor a mat, nor a bit of carpeting, but what is new. I didn't buy so much as a spoon or a paste-pin at second-hand. I had all fresh and first-rate. I made up my mind to give a good price for a good article, and I gave it. I went all the animal, the whole——'

'Yes, John Henry, yes, it is charming, but it ought to be. I have been accustomed to respectability. We always had things in good style at home. Our dining-room at Chubb Gardens is larger.'

'Not larger than this, Sarah Julia, and if it is, it is spoiled by having no light – as black as a prison. Then you've a new carriage, and the finest pair of horses in the neighbourhood.'

'Well, I ought to have, and a new pew in the new chapel. I am worth it all, am I not, John Henry?'

'If I had not thought so, you should not have had it.'

'I am the best thing you possess, new or old, after all, am I not?'

'No, that you're not.'

'Indeed, I should be glad to know what you have more precious.'

'The mill, the old mill in Foothill Road, to be sure.'

'I hate the mill; I'm ashamed of it. But after the mill?'

'You are not the next best thing after the mill.'

'Oh! John Henry.'

'Credit and connections come before you.'

'What do I care for your credit and connections?'

'You ought to care. All your good style, as you say, depend on them.'

'Well, but after?'

'You've still a rival.'

'I haven't, John. I can't have yet. We're hardly out of the honeymoon.'

'Pooh! I've known this rival five years before I ever heard the name of Sarah Julia Dobson, or went to Chubb Gardens.'

'You *shall* tell me who.'

'I've no objection – Tim Steele.'

'Your bookkeeper – dirty, greasy, ugly being! I always use my vinaigrette when he comes near me. He smells so of musty wool and rancid oil.'

'Tim is as sweet as a rose. He is a clever fellow, a real good tradesman. He learned the business in the old days with my father, and he says I'm a raight 'un, up to summit, but naught like t'owd maister.'

'Bah! Talk no more about the business. Do I come after Tim!'

'May be ay, and may be no.'

'Very well, sir, I can be as cool as you. I don't care where I come here; at home I was always first.'

'There, pout, Sarah. I hear the evening post is come and you can get over the sulky fit while I am reading my letters.'

The postman's knock at the door was followed by the entrance of a servant with the letter-bag. While Mr Moore examines its contents you and I, reader, will examine him, his lady, and his residence.

Mr Moore is a man of thirty-five, rather tall, very well made, and very well looking, light complexioned, with clear-cut, deft, neat English features, a profusion of sandy whiskers, blue eyes under lightly traced eyebrows. Small eyes, they are, but quick and restless, and emitting as they glance here and there, not broad flashes of light, but little sparkles like the glint of needlepoints. They almost make you smart again if they encounter your undefended face, they are so piercing and steely in their effect. They never dwell on an object; they rase it, almost scratch it, and pass on. He has a nicely defined mouth, a little attenuated but correctly shaped, I don't know how it is, not symmetrical; and thin as the lips are, you can well fancy a rasping oath escaping their slight curve. He looks agile, strong and restless; his hand now as it lies on the table is unconsciously clenched – indeed, he rarely has a hand, generally fists, and his elbows are perpetually squared as if he were ever thrusting his way through a densely packed, invisible crowd.

Mrs Moore looks some eight or ten years younger than her husband. In her aspect also you recognize health, vigour, physical power – excellent qualities all. She has a handsome shape now, but will be very stout by the time she is forty. Were all women shaped like Mrs Moore, bustles, etc., would never have been invented, for she needs no aid of the kind. Her face is scarcely beautiful: the nose is up-turned, the brow is low, the mouth is rather wide, but the healthy colour of her cheek and lips, the profusion of her hair, its waving curl, the advantage of a white and complete set of teeth, make a whole which deserves the epithet of handsome, or at least fine-looking; and as she sits there in her evening dress of enamel-blue poplin with trimming of white swan's-down lightly surrounding her well-made bust, she looks the most lustrous and freshest object in the room, which is not saying a little, for every stick of furniture in that room is, as Mr Moore declared, 'bran new', and the ruddy French polished mahogany, the burnished gilding, the crimson papering seem to blaze again by the light of the lamp. I have said nothing about the expression of Mrs Moore's face, and I do not mean to say much about it. It was quite good enough for Mr Moore, quite elevated, quite gentle, quite intellectual enough for him. And do not be uneasy, reader, at the introduction of those epithets. I have no intention to draw on your sympathy, to attack your heart. I give no hint of an ill-assorted union, of neglect or hard usage of a young bride by a somewhat worldly man; though the little dialogue with which I commenced was not quite so soft as the cooing of two doves in a grove, yet it is the precursor of no marital oppressions or distresses. No; be assured that Mrs Moore was a match for her husband, could hold her own, did not want the tenderness he was unapt to give, understood affection as he understood it, saw the world through much the same medium as her John Henry did, and made much the same estimate of the essentials of earthly happiness as he made.

Mr Moore before his marriage had been accustomed to say that Sarah Julia Dobson had sense; and he was right. She had the only sort of sense he was capable of appreciating – the sense of the senses, the sense of the substantial, the sense of self-interest. That last she possessed in perfection, and so did he.

Mrs Moore was the daughter of a wealthy nobleman's agent; her father had thriven in the pleasant place where his lines had been cast. He could give his handsome girls good portions. They found no difficulty consequently in making eligible matches, and not the least advantageous was the one which Sarah Julia achieved with the prosperous young manufacturer, in whose dining room we are now present.

Prosperous, Mr Moore's residence proclaimed him to be. It was one of several detached houses in the most fashionable outskirts of Everintoyle, and when I mention that well-known and affluent locality, the reader will immediately recall the picture of the many stately stone-built dwellings whose surrounding gardens and shrubberies make green and gay the environs of a place which at heart is rather black, vexed, and worried. The poplars of Aspen Place formed a verdant fringe along that broad and wheel-torn highway which merges in Foothill Road. From fields you pass to villas, from villas to gay shops, from shops you go down amid factories. They hem you in long and lofty. Their appropriate din, atmosphere, and population possess the air, echoes, and streets. Dimness, noise, and labour brood, resound, and travail in Foothill Road.

Mr Moore, having thrown into his wife's lap a note or two

with her address, proceeded to run his sharp eye over a considerable mass of business letters quicker almost than you or I, reader, could have broken the seals. It is true they were very short, but then they were numerous, and required severally a pencil-note on the margin. This note made, they were tied in a packet with red tape and put aside, to be 'work for Tim,' as the manufacturer said, with an emphatic slap on the packet. One letter yet remained, differently directed, differently folded from the others – a private letter, evidently, no business despatch.

'From Will,' said Mr Moore, as he glanced at it before opening it, and he curled his lip with an odd expression, uncordial, ungenial, reluctant. 'I know little of Will, and it's strange, I don't wish to know more of him,' he added, rather making the observation to himself than to Mrs Moore, who being engrossed with a long epistle from one of her sisters describing minutely a large party they had had at Chubb Gardens a few days since, had just then neither eyes nor ears for her husband's affairs.

'I'd rather he kept out of my way, and claimed neither relationship nor acquaintance,' he soliloquized. 'D——n me if I can quite understand it, but that fellow's style of writing is a nuisance to me. I'd as lief get nothing as his letters, and yet they're short and I suppose well expressed. If I thought I was ever to have much to do with him, the idea would annoy me. Why, I really don't know, but his bringing-up and mine have been different. His notions and mine are, I dare say, different, more so than he is aware. He always seems to think, indeed, that he and I must somehow of necessity agree. Is he what they call an affectionate lad? Affection be hanged! I hate to be bothered for or with affection – not that he bothers me; not that, in short, he ever says anything about it. But every letter he sends I always think he will, and that annoys me. I wish I could cut him. Sarah Julia, here, read this scrawl.'

'They have been coming out in grand style at home, John Henry. It was mother's birthday, and they had a dance. They might have saved their gaiety till we went to see them. Rachel Matilda describes all the dresses. Listen: mother had a yellow——'

'Stop, I won't listen – that's distinct, I hope. I know the colour of all Mrs Dobson's gowns, and of all Mr Dobson's inexpressibles, and I won't go over the catalogue unless I was paid for it, and paid well, a sovereign per article, which you can't afford. Besides, confound Chubb Gardens and "Home", and "They"! You're at Everintoyle now, and Aspen Place is your place, and I'm all the "They" you ought to think about.'

'Oh, are you? What, you're going to turn against father and mother? I call it very disrespectful to speak in that way.'

'Disrespectful or not, it's my way. You must put up with my way, you must, Sarah. You'll find you must.'

'John Henry, there never was any one so rude as you are. Mother said you were a rude man before we were married, and Rachel Matilda always declared you were no gentleman.'

'Rude or polished, I'm the only man for you, so put up with me. And, gentleman or clown, I'm your husband, July. Are you going to cry?'

'I'm sure, to be treated so, before six months – it's shameful, shameful, shameful!'

'Shameful be it. No, shameless you mean, for I never knew shame in my life.'

'I'll go home to-morrow. Dear Chubb Gardens, dear mother, dear father!'

'Go, duck.'

'Duck! I am no more of a duck than you are a drake. I won't bear such language.'

'You won't bear? Come, my lass, you shall learn to know me. Which is to be master, think you – you or I?'

'I don't care, I'll leave you.'

'Now, you've a spirit, Sarah, I know. That nose and those little brown eyes of yours are as full of contradiction and wilfulness as may be, but you'll have to give in. They've petted and spoiled you at home. I shan't spoil you.'

'No, you'll tyrannize me.'

'I'll be master, I'll be obeyed; and to begin, you'll just fold that Rachel-Matilda letter up and put it in your pocket.'

'Pocket? I've no such vulgar thing as a pocket.'

'I have two, four, so give it to me' (he took it and

sequestered it), 'and you'll read Will's letter up in an audible voice for my edification.'

'You've taken my letter; you've robbed me.'

'Robbed? A man rob his wife? What's yours is mine.'

Mrs Moore was exasperated; symptoms of hysterics began to appear. Mr Moore enjoyed it.

'That's droll,' said he. 'You don't know whether you'd laugh or cry. I'd make up my mind, if I were you.'

Mrs Moore both laughed and cried till she was well tired.

'You're a bonnie sight,' he said.

'Too good for you – a thousand times too good for you.'

'That depends on what I think. If I'd seen you set that face before we were wed, I can tell you the licence would never have been bought.'

'Vulgar man! Insolent man.'

'You look as if you had had a fit; there is not a feature in your face straight, or as it should be. Sarah Julia, when you are as old as your mother you will be like her – just as red-faced, just as fat, and she is three yards round if she's an inch.'

'If I'd only known – if I could but have foreseen!' cried Mrs Moore.

'What a devil of a man I was going to be married to,' subjoined her spouse, mimicking her voice, 'I would have died an old maid.'

'Indeed, I should not have died an old maid. Joseph Cocker was miserable for me, and so was Mr Booth. I might have had either of them for lifting my little finger. Poor Mr Booth! dear Mr Booth! Rachel Matilda says how ill he looks.'

'He would have looked much worse if he had been in my shoes. Booth was a ninny, and you would have eaten him without salt in process of time; but you'd better not try it on with me. I'd as soon advise a woman to swallow her shoeing-horn as to gulp down John Henry Moore.'

'Bad man! Bad man!'

'Come, there's the letter to read. I mean to have it read.'

'What do I care for *your* brother's letters?'

'Almost as much as I do, I dare say; but you'll be obliged to read it.'

'I will not read it. Give me my sister's, my dear sister's note.'

'Look here,' said Mr Moore, and producing the dear sister's note he put it between the tongs and held it in the fire till it was ashes. And when he had done this, he looked at Mrs Moore with a sidelong glance that had a cool gleam of the demon in it. 'Be sharp!' he ejaculated in a guttural, provincial accent. He was not playing now; he was, if not in a passion, yet disposed to do more than vex – to crush. Mrs Moore rose as if to leave the room.

'Sit down and do as you are bid.'

She hesitated.

'Do you hear me?'

She was turning coward. 'John Henry, it's too bad,' she sobbed.

'It will be worse if I am not obeyed this minute.'

She obeyed him and resumed her seat.

'Now read.'

She opened the letter. He directly snatched it from her hand.

'I'll be damned if I let you read it!'

He sat and looked at her. Frightened she was, but not quite so much as to content him in the mood which was now roused.

'You may be off to your chamber,' he said. 'You've learned a lesson; it shall be rather sharper another time if needed, but you're too hard and buxom and clever a girl to feel the thing as I should like you to feel it. If some women were in your place just now I would carry it on farther. I would have some fun.'

'Queer sort of fun,' she said.

'Yes, July, but it's my fun. Are you frightened?'

'Frightened? I never expected this – never, never, never.'

'Pooh! Such a rosy, saucy thing as you feels nothing.'

'Feels nothing? My feelings are torn——'

'To shreds, and there's an end of 'em. I like you all the better, Sarah, for being toughish. You'll bear the sort of life I mean to lead you. You'll get used to me and I to you, but swamp the Chubb Gardens people. Sink Father Dobson, and Mother Dobson, and Sister Rachel, and all that sort of schoolgirl twaddle. If you don't intend us to quarrel daily – cut them!'

'Well, such improper, such shocking language! Such ideas——'

'What! you're off at a tangent again. Go upstairs – away.'

And away Mrs Moore went, sobbing audibly. Hers was one of those nettle tempers which are very troublesome and stinging if touched lightly, but which squeeze tame as dock leaves under an undaunted finger and thumb. To reason and gentleness she would have been often intractable; to a rough kind of despotism she was likely to be compliant enough.

John Henry laughed a dry laugh to himself when he was alone. He dubbed her 'a fine lass' in his thoughts, however, and had a very good opinion of his own prowess in vanquishing such a handsome shrew. 'Never yet knew the character that could bear up against me,' he meditated. 'When I was courting Sarah I often noticed how she swaggered over all about her at home, and I used to promise myself the pleasure of breaking her in. I knew I could do it. She may rake the servants fore and aft if she will, but she *shall* obey me; and then as long as she's young and I'm young, and as long as trade goes pretty well, and I've no great losses and crosses to make me cantankerous – to put me up to that temper when I can't be satisfied without having somebody to torment, to grind, to – to squeeze the life out of – we shall rub on famously; and even if the contrary happened, I should show less of the devil with her than with a white-faced, delicate little woman. Such a one as I remember William's mother was, my stepmother. Eh, what a stepson she had in me! And my father being a hard drinker, and a real Moore every inch of him – that is to say, a blackguard – there could not have been much compatibility of disposition. I wouldn't have a wife of that sort, I know that. Now, is Will like his mother? Let's look at his letter. Humph! I hate his handwriting – it's not clerkly, your gentleman's hieroglyphics these, not an Everintoyle counting-house stroke in the page. What has he to say?'

The letter commenced thus:–

'DEAR JOHN, – I and the Seacombes will never agree. I must get rid of the yoke of their patronage; it is cutting a furrow in my neck. They are good people – I allow that – and especially, singularly proper people, and I am not aware that I am either a bad or an improper person myself. Yet I cannot live with them, and I cannot breathe under them. I say breathe under them, for whenever I am in their company they seem to be sitting, literally sitting, upon my chest. There is not a vital organ, neither heart, nor lungs, nor anything else can have free play under that pressure. We never shall agree, I repeat it; impossible for me to think as they think; difficult, even most difficult, to talk as they talk, and I despise myself whenever I try the experiment. They wish, as Mr and Mrs Seacombe said to me the other day, to form my character, direct my pursuits, select my position – all this would be accomplished. They further told me, could I but be induced to study, copy, follow Dr M'Shone – You don't know M'Shone: I do, and I would not resemble him, I would not do as he does nor be what he is for his large income, his handsome wife, and his universal popularity.

'He may be sincere, but he does not look sincere. He may be bent on doing good, but the impression produced on me when I hear him preach is that he chiefly desires to excite admiration. Many accordingly admire him; I utterly dislike his style and generally his matter. The man is perched on a pedestal which no human being, and especially no human being of his stamp, ought to occupy. His congregation regard him as an angel, a god. I dare say he half despised them for their fanaticism at first, but he found the consequences of the illusion so pleasant that his sole aim is now to maintain it. This forces him into hypocrisy, and he is a hypocrite. To see him walking the streets with his chin a little elevated, his eyes half-shut, a perennial simper on his mouth, you could not for a moment mistake him for an honest, genuine character. He is a permanent actor – irksome trade.

'Mrs Seacombe worships him. Mr Seacombe, whom he calls his right hand, who is his deacon and what not, holds him as the first of authorities, the most infallible of counsellors. He is a frequent guest in Clare Street, because Mrs Seacombe has a clever cook and keeps an excellent table. She and the cook are always laying their heads together to devise something specially delicate and dainty for the doctor's eating, and as he is a consummate epicure their labour is not lost. You should see him sitting large (he is corpulent as a whale) before the fine dishes, his eyes roaming over the table, his mouth watering, and his tongue meantime ringing the changes on religious topics. He *can* take and *does* take a considerable quantity of wine, and as Mr Seacombe does the same, they suit each other. I once observed to Mrs S. that both her husband and the preacher were too convivial for religious men, and that I thought it would become them better to join a Temperance Society and take the pledge. Mrs S. received the suggestion very ill, and I don't think she has ever forgiven me for it. I remember she expressed an opinion that Temperance Societies were profane institutions, calculated to sap the foundations of true religion, and I asked her to prove it, but she could not. When Dr M'Shone has taken a certain amount of glasses, he always recurs to one theme, and that is the adulterous union of Church and State. From his ire or his subject springs an anticipation which he never fails to express, that the day is fast coming when Establishments shall be rased, and when the magnificent aisles of —— Minster shall be as free to the Sectarians as they are now to the Episcopalians; when he, M'Shone, shall sit on the Archbishop's throne and preach from the Dean's pulpit. "Yes," he says, "I trust yet to give out a hymn of Watt's from that very eminence," and then he quotes:

> "'I lift my banner, saith the Lord,
> Where Antichrist hath stood;
> The city of my gospel foes
> Shall be a field of blood.
> My heart has studied just revenge,
> And now the day appears,
> The day of my redeemed is come
> To wipe away their tears.
>
> Slaughter and my devouring sword
> Shall walk the streets around;
> Babel shall reel beneath my stroke
> And stagger to the ground.'"

'When he has had a moderate tumbler of brandy and water, he
usually cites another set of stanzas:

    "'Adore and tremble, for our God
       Is a consuming fire;
       His jealous eyes His wrath inflame
       And raise His fury higher.

       Almighty vengeance, how it burns!
       How bright His fury glows!
       Vast magazines of plagues and storms
       He treasures for His foes.

       Yet mighty God [*Here the doctor's voice grows solemnly unctious.*]
       Thy sovereign grace
       Sits right on the throne
       The refuge of Thy *chosen* race. [*What an emphasis on chosen!*]
       When wrath comes rushing down!

       Thy hand shall on rebellious kings
       A fiery tempest pour;
       While we beneath Thy sheltering wings
       Thy just revenge adore."

'So moved was I the first time I heard these stanzas that at the
close I exclaimed "flat blasphemy." Whereupon Mr Seacombe
requested me to quit the table, which I did very willingly.

    'Now, John, you will begin to wonder why I am writing
you such a long rambling letter, and indeed it is time I came
to the point, for I have a point in all this. I want your advice,
perhaps your help, in a certain matter. You know what my
vocation has been till now – sub-editor of the *Westhaven
Oracle*. Allow me to whisper to you that I am mortally sick of
this vocation. The *Westhaven Oracle* is the organ of a bigoted
sect and a narrow-minded party. I am perpetually called upon
to advocate principles I despise, or rather, to advocate them in
a manner I despise. It is not the principles which are so far
wrong as the feeling of those who hold the principles – an

intolerant, a proselytizing, a meddling, an envious feeling; a feeling which is not satisfied with conscientious faithfulness in the exposition of doctrine, the maintenance of principles, which is not content with truth, with candour, nor even with honest zeal, but which will exact violence, abuse of opponents, craving and godless ambition after distinctions and privileges which it at once decries and covets for itself. Religious discussion, I find, is my aversion; political discussion (at least in the only fashion which is permitted in the *Westhaven Oracle*) no less so. I cannot for my life believe in any political leader; I cannot be a thorough-going party man to any side. When I know that a certain systematic course of opposition is factious, when I see that a certain pretended philanthropy is hollow, I cannot honestly maintain the opposition or cry up the philanthropy. As far as my experience goes I have ever found self-interest all dominant and all influential, alike in the Church, Convocation, and in the electioneering committee. I would not care so much if it would call itself by its proper name and show its natural face honestly, but it assumes so many aliases and wears so many masks, that at last I am determined to eschew it. A sub-editor I will be no longer. I have told Mr Calvert so much. To my astonishment he seemed gratified at the announcement. He said that both he and Dr Greatorix, and most of the leading subscribers to the *Oracle*, and members of Bethesda Chapel, had long wished me to resign the editorship; they thought I had scarcely that nerve and decision which the times demanded, that I was too young for the post, and so on. Another career had been thought of for me, he said, and he was convinced it would suit me better. I asked what. The office of the ministry – I had talents, Dr Greatorix allowed that. Dr Greatorix recommended that I should take two years' training at Rawdale College, and then Dr Greatorix would accept me as assistant. Dr Greatorix would give me the benefit of his shining example. If I succeeded and became that privileged instrument which Dr G. anticipated and believed I should become, Dr G. had ulterior views for me of the most benignant and munificent nature.

'Here Mr Calvert arrested his revelations. I pressed for further enlightenment. What, I asked, were these ulterior views? With difficulty I extorted two mystic hints: putting them together, and cogitating upon them, I made out the plan double-barrelled – of getting a harmonious call for me to the new chapel it is in contemplation to erect in the suburbs, and marrying me to Miss Hester Greatorix, Dr Greatorix's niece.

'When this binary ray of intelligence smote my soul, I instantly took a chair. I felt too drunk with glory to stand. A preacher in Bethesda Chapel! The husband of Hester Greatorix! Far too much honour for one mortal that. Some have greatness thrust upon them indeed.

'I have no intention of being insolent in speaking of Miss Greatorix, but I could no more marry her than I could marry my grandmother if she were now living. I can hardly tell you why I have this feeling – at least I cannot tell you without reflecting upon it. It is not because she is so very old; for though she is upwards of thirty, and I am but twenty-five, this difference of age is not the cause of my repugnance. It is not on account of her disposition or education – both are very good. It is not owing to her circumstances – they are prosperous. In a pecuniary point of view she would be considered a prize for a penniless man like me. It is, I believe, because she jars upon me in every sense. Her look, her face, her shape, her gait, her voice – all jar on my nerves, optic or auricular. Her opinions, her sentiments, jar on mine. She is rather tall, not in the least deformed, but curiously inharmonious. I have often sat looking at her large head, her rather long and thick neck, her narrow shoulders, thin frame, and long arms, with a stupid amazement that Nature should have put together anything so discordant. I have watched the movements of her large feet, when she walks, with pain. I have listened to her deep and long-drawn voice, when she speaks and reads, with stupor. Her style of reading is indeed nameless. She has her perfect senses; there is nothing idiotic about her. Why, in God's name, then, does she not read differently? Oh, the protracted agony of her tones lingering on Scripture phrases! A chapter in the Bible handled, I mean mouthed, by her is a bit of purgatory. Listening, you bow your face and cover it with your hands ashamed for her. Nevertheless, Hester has her good points. She is a better, because a more sincere, woman than her uncle is a man. I respect her, but to undertake to love or to marry her is what the rack could not force me to do.

'And salt whips and scourges of scorpions should not transform me into a student of Rawdale, much less a minister of Bethesda. In modified terms I expressed these resolutions to Mr Calvert. He was angry, indignant; so was Dr Greatorix: in short, we can assimilate no longer. I must change my ground, seek a new business in a new place, and I want to come to Everintoyle. Can you do with me as a clerk in your counting-house? If you have a vacancy, try me. You will find me industrious at the least. I scarcely know you personally, John, for we have been separated from boyhood, but as my half-brother (an entire brother in my thoughts) you are the nearest relation I have. I have expressed myself to you, then, with confidence. I am sure you will understand me, and I believe you will help me if you can. Let me have an answer at your earliest convenience. – I am, your affectionate brother,

'WILLIAM CALVERT MOORE.'

John Henry Moore having read this letter, laughed. His laugh over, he bit his thin lips and reflected. Then he said –

'I'll be his master, I see I can. He's a sop.' Again he mused; looking hard at the fire, he exclaimed, 'I'll have him,' twisted his chair round to the table, seized pen, ink, and paper, and scribbled:–

'DEAR BILL, – I don't admire your worldly wisdom. A rich marriage would have been better than a poor clerkship, but since you prefer the latter you may try it. I don't expect to find much of the tradesman in you; however, I believe you have a smattering of French and German that will suit the foreign correspondence of the house. You may come next week, if you like. Don't expect an extravagant salary; I can't afford high wages to a novice. – Yours truly,

J. H. MOORE.'

## CHAPTER II

Mr and Mrs Moore made up their quarrel, but before the lady (who I have hinted was, on the whole, a match for the gentleman) would quite come round, entirely relinquish a scheme she had formed for packing up a few things and starting by the next day's coach for Chubb Gardens, she stipulated for permission to invite 'a friend' to stay with her for some weeks, alleging that Aspen Place was dreadfully dull, and that during the hours John Henry was at the mill, she did not know 'how to put time on.'

John Henry revolted at first. Of all things he hated the idea of 'a friend', a lady friend, coming and staying, or 'stopping' as he phrased it, a his house. 'What they came for he could not tell – to eat and drink at other people's expense, he supposed, to show their fine clothes off, to catch husbands. He wished women only knew how little men really cared for them, how they saw through their arts, what a trifle a dressed-up young Miss sitting in state waiting to be married was in their eyes. He just wished they knew it – that was all.'

Mrs Moore affirmed that if ladies knew ever so well what men thought, they would not care. 'Perhaps,' she suggested, with some pungency, 'women thought quite as little of them as they thought of women. What, did John Henry suppose, could be women's opinion of men when they saw them spending half their time in smoking nasty cigars and drinking bottled liquids of different kinds. By-the-bye, John Henry,' she proceeded, 'you had far too much brandy and water last night yourself, and I know that you and Tim Steele keep spirits and porter in the counting-house. If I had only known six months ago as much as

I do now! But, independently of that, men in general are not so much idolised by women as you think. You gentlemen are all of you intensely conceited: you fancy you may do anything, make as great nuisances of yourselves as you please, and yet be worshipped. But you are mistaken.'

'Woman are hypocrites.'

'Hypocrites? No, men are hypocrites; they pretend to be so smooth and good when they want anything. And they are – but it's of no use saying what they are. And then to be on any decent terms with you, one must dissemble. If we scold you for your bad ways, you turn furious, and you have the upper hand in law, and in everything. I am sick of life.'

'What a regular vixen you are, running on in this way when I've not said a word. But it is good fun to hear you. Only mind you must attend to times and seasons, for if you were to attack me in this way after I have been making a bad bargain, or got word that a creditor has broken, or after a strike of the hands, or any other annoyance, I should——'

'Oh, I know what you would do, you need not tell me. I won't be threatened. Now, may Miss Whinn come?'

'She may come and be d——d, only mind, Sarah, she's never to sit in my chair, and she's not to touch the newspapers in a morning till I've read them. What I hate in she-visitors is, they are always sitting down prim and settled in seats that don't belong to them. Enter the room when you may, they are sure to have got the comfortable nook in the chimney-corner, and then they seize your book or your journal, and you never feel as if you were your own man for their encroachments.'

'May she come?'

'I have answered you. Ask me again and I'll say no.'

Thus the point was settled, and Miss Whinn came a day or two before William Moore was expected.

Now Miss Whinn thought she performed an act of great condescension in coming 'to stop' at a manufacturer's house in Everintoyle, for her father was not in business. He was a squire, a magistrate, had landed property, and had long ago made a point of forgetting that his own father had been a cotton-spinner, and his grandfather a working wool-comber. Miss

Whinn had had a year's finish at a school in Kensington, where Miss S.J. Dobson had been finished also. She was the youngest and prettiest and most petted child of her parents; she was likely to have a handsome fortune, she had an acquired prejudice against mills and mill-owners, trade and tradesmen, and an inherent hankering after something in the aristocratic line. In short, she had tastes of a soaring and refined kind (as she thought). Consequently Everintoyle, huge, wealthy, laborious place as it was, was a despicable spot in her eyes. She always called it 'a horrible hole' when she spoke of it, and her reasons for consenting now to pay a visit there were, firstly, because De Walden Hall (her father's residence, formerly called Walldean after a steep hill which rose behind it, but rechristened of late years) was an intensely dull place, as Mr Whinn was too superior to his neighbours to be on visiting terms with them; secondly, because Miss Whinn possessed, in her own estimation, accomplishments and manners above what was common in Everintoyle, and expected to show off there; and thirdly, because she reckoned upon much amusement in distressing the hearts of the young mill-owners. Mrs Moore had not failed to tell her, when she wrote the invitation, that a brother of Mr Moore's was likely to be resident in the house during her stay, and this piquant circumstance had decided her otherwise somewhat vacillating resolution.

Now, reader, you have had explanation enough, and as a change you shall presently have a little description.

This is the day on which William Moore is expected to arrive at Aspen Place, a wet, winter day. It has been so wet all the morning that Mrs John Henry and Miss Wynne (it used to be written Whinn) have been kept prisoners, and they have spent the whole time from breakfast till dinner in talking about the 'Coming Man'. The young matron has not failed to appraise the young maiden that 'Mr William' has no fortune, not a farthing, that he is quite dependent on his own exertions. Consequently, as a serious matrimonial speculation, he is altogether ineligible, and Miss Wynne, after declaring that if he had mountains of gold it would be all the same to her, as no amount of wealth could ever induce her to marry a person in business, or who thought of going into business, has made up her mind to the damping circumstance of his being without a penny.

Evening is closed; the cloth is laid in the dining-room. When the kitchen door is opened, a savoury smell steals from it along the passage announcing dinner nearly ready. Half an hour since Mr Moore came in from the mill, and a gentleman with him. Both are now upstairs. They have not seen the ladies, who were dressing when they arrived. This is the little drawing-room, reader. I see there a good fire, and the lamp is lit. Step in. No one is come down as yet; take that quaint little ebony chair with the wreath of roses, tulips, and lilies worked on its cushioned back, amuse yourself with this book of engravings, portraits of celebrated characters. Here is the Duke of Wellington. I always like to see his face; I am never tired of seeing it. I will believe the Duke of Wellington is both a good and a great man. He is very stern-looking, you will say, but still there is something good-humoured in his sternness; his heart is perhaps guarded by an iron case. But I do not believe the contents of that case are metallic. And here is Lord John Russell. I like Lord John Russell again – little ugly soul. There are lines of feeling as well as of care in his physiognomy. I should hate to hear of that man being cruelly set upon by a party, and torn and bailed and worried to death. Politicians seem to think nothing of the human being when they turn savage, and in this case the human being deserves to be thought of. Sir Robert Peel! One's heart does not warm to him so much, because he has not a very sincere look. We are not, however, going to run over a long list of celebrated personages; indeed, ere we have glanced through half the volume our eyes are attracted to something else.

A figure comes gliding into the drawing-room, a girl in a light evening dress, a fair and pretty girl, with white neck, white shoulders, white hands and arms. She wears a bracelet on one wrist; a little gold chain traces a delicately gleaming circle round her throat; her hair is dressed in a somewhat peculiar fashion – a fashion not unbecoming, but a little fantastic. The mode has been studied after a picture, and so has the arrangement of her scarf.

This is Miss Wynne, reader. Look at her well. She is pretty to look at, with her blonde hair and complexion, and she thinks so, for perceiving the apartment to be empty, she steps up to a mirror and surveys her reflected person. It is a gratifying spectacle. She throws her head now to this side, now that; she makes her hair wave; she raises her arm and curves it in various attitudes; she adjusts and readjusts her drapery. Deeply content with the result of each experiment, she makes a profound curtsy before the charming image, gracefully retires, and sinks into a chair. Here she assumes a 'pose', her head inclined to one side droops upon her left hand, her right holds loosely a small, elegant volume, which she seems to have been perusing, her handkerchief has fallen at her feet. Of what is she musing? A word or two uttered with some vehemence partly informs us.

'*Would* that I had been called Alicia de Walden instead of Alice Wynne! But Alicia I will be – that I am resolved!' And, depend upon it, when Alice or Alicia Wynne has resolved upon a thing she usually accomplishes it. For sentimental or fragile as she is (or would like to be thought), there is something in that chin of hers (a rather large and decided chin in proportion to her other features) which announces a practical character, quite qualified to push its way where advance is desired.

Mrs Moore comes in, well dressed and well favoured as usual. She has her faults, as we have seen, but she looks a more honest person than Miss Wynne. Alicia starts up.

'My dear Julia, how do I look? I fear I am quite a fright this evening.'

Mrs Moore reassures her by a civil speech.

'Is that wretch the future clerk come?'

'What, William Moore? Yes, he came in with John some time since.'

'The wretch!' again cries Alicia. (She piques herself on a certain extraordinary emphasis both in her choice of words, and often in her tone of speaking, though this vigour is not held inconsistent with changes of interesting langour.) 'I positively hate him already; the man puts me in quite a flutter. What is he like? Have you seen him?'

'Not yet, but he is coming. No, it is only John Henry.'

'Mr Moore, where is your brother?'

'Donning himself,' replied Mr Moore, who delighted to be as rough, as provincial, nay, as coarse, as he well could be, when conversing with Miss Wynne, because he hated her, knowing that she hated him.

'*Donning* himself?' she repeated, turning up the whites of her eyes.

'Yes, he was as wet as a ratton. He rid on the top of the coach all the way from Westhaven, and it's a middling spell of road. So I said, doff that coat and them – them other garments, Bill, before you come in to dinner, as we have a young lady stopping here who has made up her mind to wed you, and you'd better dash in smart before her at once.'

'Dear Mr Moore, have you a cold? Your voice is most nasal, and guttural likewise, more so even than usual. Do you know, Julia, I can never understand above half of what your husband says, there's so strong a tinge of the Doric in his language.'

'Naught equal to your father, mun; he's the capper for a raight north country tongue. And as to old Jacky Whin, your grandfather, he spake i' this fashion: Aw wold ha' gaanged a gaiters wi' him ower t' brace if he'd nobbut a sotten a two three minits longer i' th' hod, which means – Sarah, what does it mean? You understand ——shire well enough. Translate for Miss Alice.'

'For shame, John Henry! How insupportably rude you are!'

'Nothing of the kind, it does not mean that. Your great-grandfather, Miss Wynne, was a wool-comber, and he used to work for my grandfather, who built the first mill in Kenneldale, where both your ancestors and mine lived. The Moores have always been villains as far as I can trace them up, and very fond of making money either by fair means or foul. Well, Billy Moore, my old grandsire, and the Fosters and the Pighills and the Ramsdens – you've heard of them all, though your folks don't visit with them now. They were the old gentry of the Dale – became concerned and allied once upon a time in an affair which history has not clearly defined, but which was illegal. They were a pack of ignorant boars, the whole set, and did not very well know what they were about, or what risks they ran, but they made Jacky Whin their tool and ambassador, and he was taken up and sent to —— Castle. We've both reason to be proud of our blood, haven't we, Miss Wynne?'

'I know nothing of the persons or transactions to which you allude. I congratulate you on your ancestor's share in them. Julia, this little confined room of yours is insufferably close.'

'Shall I leave the door open then?' asked another voice, and the speaker entering approached the fire.

'You've been three-quarters of an hour in dressing, Bill,' exclaimed Mr Moore, pulling out his watch. 'A glorious beginning! What a clerk you'll make, what a man of business! my word.'

'This is your lady, I suppose, John?' said the stranger, offering his hand to Mrs Moore.

'Exactly, and this is the rose of De Walden Hall. Do you remember, William. You've been there when you were a brat, and it was a farmhouse. An old dame Whin, this Miss Alicia's grandmother, used to give you bread and treacle, with which you made a sight of yourself and your bib.'

'I have forgotten the bib, but I do dimly remember something about the bread and treacle, and more distinctly that you, John, used to snatch my share from me.'

'I dare say, I was always up to snuff.'

'Are you in that line still? Does he still act on the principle of appropriating more than his right, Mrs Moore?'

'He will take all he can get.'

'Yes, might is right, that's my motto, and now come to dinner. Oh, with what pride and pleasure Miss Alice takes my arm, and for love of the good old martyr of Kenneldale I give it her with the same feelings. Bill, bring t' mistress.'

We will not follow them to the dining-room, as we could take but an ideal share of the repast there set forth. We will rejoin them an hour or two later, when they are once more all in the drawing-room. Mr Moore is now dropping asleep in the easy-chair, which he has taken good care to get possession of before Miss Wynne could assume it. Mrs Moore sits by the table near the lamp, deep in fancy work. Mr William and Miss Alicia are sitting near, and at intervals looking at each other.

William Moore considers Miss Wynne very pretty. He is thinking how much more symmetrical are her proportions than those of poor Hester Greatorix, but he wonders at something about her, something in her movements, her mode of speaking, which strikes him as *outré*. She is always changing her attitude, she always speaks as if she expected people to discover that there was a marked point in what she says. This point he cannot find, and he is pondering to discover it.

Miss Alicia, meantime, dislikes his spectacles, which prevent her from seeing exactly where his eye is fixed, and she thinks him *outré* too. And indeed William Moore is rather peculiar.

He is middle-sized, spare and wiry, but proportionate in figure. There is little or no resemblance in him to his brother. He has none of John's sanguine temperament. The manufacturer's orange whiskers, sandy hair, fresh complexion, alert look, neat, regular features, are not to be traced in the ex-editor's thin visage, in his rather dark, pale, and nervous aspect, of which the chief point is a large forehead. The ordinary nose and grave mouth are neither ugly nor handsome; the eyes are very dark grey, large, and deep-set, and just now, when he has taken off his glasses an instant, you see they have a wistful light in them difficult to describe, but which suits a certain patient sternness or stern patience to my thinking, the fixed characteristic of his other features. He can see scarcely anything without spectacles, for he is short-sighted as an owl; but you would say he thought he saw much. Fitful gleams, not of vision but emotion, inform his irises, dilate his pupils now as he sits looking at nothing – 'William, put your glasses on again. Miss Alicia thinks you a very strange being, far from handsome, and I can assure you your comely sister-in-law deems you immeasurably inferior to her John Henry. That is right – in spectacles you have a more knowing appearance, you look less dreamy, better fitted to push your way through the world. Is that a satirical expression playing round your mouth? I believe it is, indeed I have no doubt of it. I shall not trouble myself to be anxious about you, nor need any one else; careworn and thoughtful as you look, you look keen and quizzical too.'

'Now, Mr William,' cries Miss Alicia suddenly, and with that impulsive manner she seems to think it becoming to affect, 'how do you expect to get on in this horrid Everintoyle? Surely you don't consider the place congenial?'

'Quite so. My aim is to make money, and Everintoyle is said to offer good facilities for that.'

'To make money! And is that your highest aim? Oh, how grovelling! Were I a man I would strive after something higher than that.'

'Would you?' said Mr William abstractedly; and he added soon, 'The lower rounds of the ladder must be mounted ere the top can be reached.'

'Oh, with proper energy one might jump to the top at once,' cried Miss Wynne, who wished rather to shine than to hear or communicate sense.

'A mountebank who is used to vaulting might do it,' was the reply; 'an ordinary aspirant must rise with more caution. He must earn money that he may be able to look up to the higher blessings of life.'

'What are the higher blessings?'

'Time is one. You cannot be master of your time without a competency, and time is necessary to think, to plan, to execute.'

'To think, plan, execute what? Oh dear, how slow you are!'

'Any project worth realising.'

'Have you any projects in your head?'

'I am no speculator, no theorist.'

'You are of the class of plodders, perhaps?'

'Perhaps I am; my views plod rather than soar. I confine them at present to a clerk's place, duties and salary.'

Alicia curled her lip. She felt a sort of contempt for this grave young embryo trader. It was not easy to say what he felt for her. He seemed used to command both his feelings and his face. There was a pause of some minutes, during which William Moore looked alternately at Miss Wynne, his brother, and his sister-in-law. No muscle of his features moved while he surveyed them, and the scrutiny over, you saw that he withdrew into himself, that he locked something, opinions or feelings, in his breast as effectively and quickly as if he had been enclosing gold in a casket. You perceived too, by a superficial clearing of his countenance, that he left out some unimportant sentiments and notions to serve as a fund for present light parley, as you might exclude from the strong box a handful of small change for temporary expenses.

'Do you sing?' he asked, turning briskly to Alicia.

'Sing? Oh pray, Julia, answer for me.'

Mrs Moore, of course, eulogised her guest's powers. Miss Wynne was both a songstress and a musician. Immediately William Moore rose, opened the piano with alacrity, led the lady to it. The first notes woke John Henry. He sat staring at her a few minutes while she played the air. No sooner did her voice blend with the accompaniment than he informed his wife he 'could never stand this', and left the room. 'Evening Chimes' or 'Morning Chimes', at any rate chimes of some date, was the burden of the song. The performer had a small and weak voice, which was managed with some art and more artifice. She intended to be thought to sing with feeling and expression. Not possessing the first, however, she could not gain the last. Various canzonettes followed 'the chimes'. Her auditor walked about patiently at the farthest end of the drawing-room. At last she struck into 'Rousseau's Dream'. He uttered a slight groan to himself. 'Not that, I love that,' he said softly. He seemed about to approach and arrest her, but checked himself smiling, and sitting down near his sister-in-law's table, he seized a work-basket. He dived recklessly among the contents as the song proceeded.

'Put it down,' said Mrs Moore. 'You are unwinding my reels and entangling my silks; you are worse than John Henry.'

'Oh, tell your friend to cease singing,' he whispered, 'my head aches.'

'Nonsense! How can I do that? That is just like my husband. Are you as much of a young-lady-hater as he is?'

'A young-lady-hater? I don't know. If you had said a woman-hater I should have understood you. I am no woman-hater. I love, I mean I esteem women when they are in any point what I think women should be. But you are modelled by education or something else into strange beings, you women.'

'You are a strange being, I think!' said Mrs Moore, tossing her head and opening her eyes.

'I believe I am,' was the answer, 'with strange tastes. Mrs Calvert always says I am destined to be an old bachelor. Do you think I am, Mrs Moore?'

'I don't know, I shouldn't wonder – most likely. What is your opinion, Alicia, do you think Mr William here looks like a marrying man?'

'Has he directed you to ask?'

'He has been inquiring.'

'Then tell him no, positively no. Clerks cannot presume to think of marrying.'

'Oh, but they will presume to think of marrying. For my part, I shall certainly marry one day, if I live,' answered William quietly. He did everything quietly; he spoke, looked, moved without bustle. You began to feel he was decidedly a quiet man. Perhaps Miss Alicia did not like quiet men, or it might be she did not like quizzical men, for William was as indisputably one as the other. Perhaps she was offended that he had not stood behind her while she sang, and turned the leaves of her music-book; perhaps the circumstance of his not having praised her singing annoyed her; perhaps she had a general impression that she could not influence him, that he remained cool in the glow of her charms. At any rate she replied with haughty emphasis.

'You mean you will marry one of your own class.'

'Ah, just so. I assure you I shall marry none other.'

'A very prudent resolve.'

'A proud one, you mean. That is the insanity, the impracticability of it. I look too high, and as I won't descend one inch, I may after all be doomed to celibacy.'

Miss Wynne raised her eyebrows and her shoulders, and interchanged a meaning glance with Mrs Moore. The latter, who was an honest if a blunt woman, one who never repressed her sentiments, exclaimed –

'Upon my word, you have some conceit in you!'

'Not more than is requisite, none that I can afford to part with.'

'Will you define your class?' said Miss Alicia. 'We are not romancing, are we? We don't sit in the presence of a prince in disguise?'

'Will *you* define my class?' he asked.

'Oh, the feminine of clerk,' she began meditatively. 'Governess, is it, milliner? Mercer? What else?'

'It might be maid-servant,' returned the imperturbable ex-editor. 'Fate and the Future alone know in what degree of the social scale my treasure exists. But I expect to find the face I shall wish to kiss rather under a plain straw bonnet than under one of velvet. I shall look amongst the pale, busy, thrifty ranks trained by Adversity and Labour rather than amongst the untried, untaught daughters of Luxury and Ease. Certain plants grow only in trodden ways. It were waste of time to seek them in hothouses.'

'John Henry will not be pleased if you marry a girl without money, and it is mere ruin to any man to connect himself with a poor family,' said Mrs Moore. 'When your brother was coming to Chubb Gardens, people said what an advantage it was to his credit, and how it strengthened his connection to have it known that he was looking where there was a fortune. I don't mean to boast, but everyone said so. And you see father and mother want for nothing, and they never trouble him with begging or borrowing.'

'John did quite right to seek your hand, my dear madam, but if I were to apply for your sister's, I should do very wrong.'

'That you would; Rachel Matilda wouldn't have you.'

'How do you know?'

'Because I know I wouldn't have you myself if I were single.'

'Why? You are frank and truthful, Mrs John, tell me why — on account of my look?'

'Partly that, and partly your circumstances. You can't marry with a clerk's salary.'

William mused and said nothing.

'Can you now?' she urged.

'I could not marry *you*, my dear sister, if you were still to be married.'

Mrs Moore was not herself either of a refined or a gentle nature. She was a blunt, plain, positive person. She could be acrimonious; she could, when she dared, be a termagant. Her susceptibilities were not acute, they knew no soft and sweet, no vivid and subtle varieties of impression. Yet even Mrs Moore heard something in William's deep, mild voice as he now spoke, that claimed a friendly rather than a harsh feeling for the speaker, and she received something from the present moment's expression of his features which made her content that he should have addressed her as his dear sister. Alicia, less genuine, if more cultivated than Sarah Julia, lost both the tone and look.

'What do you mean by so pointedly saying you could not marry Mrs Moore?' she asked in her tart, hard style, a style which she believed, and which some others believed, to be clever and brilliant.

'Because my sister has been accustomed to comfort and affluence from her childhood, and she would need the indulgences affluence gives more than you would, Miss Wynne.'

'More than I? More than I?' cried Alicia, and she gasped at the clerk's audacity.

'Yes, you are of a harder, a more wiry nature than she.'

'I hard? wiry?'

'You could bear a great deal. If you had been born poor you would have been a working, saving personage, very saving. You would have stinted yourself of sugar in your tea all the week to have laid by sufficient to purchase a smart bonnet for Sunday. You would have carried a sovereign to the savings bank now and then. When you married, you would have been able to bring into your husband's cottage a chest of drawers and a clock. As soon as the children were old enough, you would have sent them to the mill, and made them work, and looked well after their earnings.'

'What queer nonsense!' interrupted Mrs Moore. Alicia could not speak for very wrath, and for amazement, too. By virtue of what faculty did this insolent, *ci-devant* printer (she confounded a little the departments of a newspaper office), this unlicked cotton-spinner (she equally confounded those of a factory), read the nature of her race? How did he know that Mrs Wynne, her mother, was a model of a domestic screw, that the economy of

De Walden Hall was conducted on as narrow a scale as it could be consistently with the maintenance of certain showy appearances? How could he divine Alicia's own besetting sin, the wish to save, to stint, the hatred to give? And on this point Mrs Moore's astonishment equalled her guest's. She and Miss Wynne had been schoolfellows. Schoolfellows have opportunities for seeing each other in their true colours. She remembered Alicia's propensity to monopolize whatever was her own, to share in what belonged to others; she recollected how she grudged to give, how she wheedled to partake. When the young ladies received presents from home – cakes or sweetmeats – she, Mrs Moore, and others of the girls ate largely of their own allotment, but they gave freely also, at least to particular friends. Alicia indulged more sparingly, made her treat last longer than some of her companions, but she more rarely than any gave. When she did give, it was on calculation to those from whom she knew she should receive back thirtyfold.

Mrs Moore then knew that her dear Miss Wynne was a niggard, but how did William Moore know it? He hadn't been at school with her; she had never come and favoured on him when he was eating a tart; she had never stood coaxing him, patting his shoulder, and kissing his cheek, when he was turning over the treasures of his trinket-box, or arranging his freshest sashes and scarfs, and his prettiest dresses in his wardrobe. Most certainly she had not flattered and petted him till he had given her his satin dancing-shoes, or his tiny Trinchinopoly gold chain, the present of an Indian uncle, or his Chinese ivory fan, or his coral necklace, or his only ring of pearl and turquoise. These things considered, Mrs Moore deemed herself justified in asking brusquely –

'How do you know she's a miser?'

William leaned his head down on his arm, which Mrs Moore's work-table supported, and laughed a silent laugh at the unsophisticated abruptness of the query, till his ears, his face were fired crimson. The fact was, he had dived into Alicia's eyes and seen covetousness at the bottom of them. He had run his glance along her features and felt where the illiberal heart gave harshness to their outline, narrowness to their significance. Some people never see anything but the bodies of those they converse with. Give them fair and fresh colour, graceful form; give them youth, give them gaiety, and they think they have got all heart can desire. But others behold almost at a glance the soul as well as the frame, the contents as well as the case; and however bright and lovely the physical part may be, if the mental is dim, gaunt, ungenial, false, chilly, pallid, morbid, sour, sullen – they are dissatisfied, and refuse to prize the flower whose bright calyx leaf holds no perfume.

William Moore, defective in actual vision, had at times a second sight which showed him his acquaintance at once in the spirit and in the flesh. That faculty was stronger on him at some moments than at others. To-night he enjoyed it freely; he saw the fine forms of the two ladies in his presence, and he saw something else – a nameless entity accompanying each material shape. This abstraction was honest and healthy, if vulgar, in Sarah Julia's case; in Alicia's it was wrinkled, frigid, and sordid. Her young figure cast on the wall for him an old and ghastly shadow. Critics, if you ever read this, do not misunderstand me, do not say I am writing about figments, or giving you a hero possessed of the Highland second sight. That is not what I mean. Perhaps some of you have the power yourselves; if so, you will seize my intent at once; if otherwise, I had better not force it on you.

Alicia Wynne felt that night that she could not make William Moore fall in love with her, that her design to fascinate him was baffled. With what malice she spoke of him to her friend when he left the room, summoned by a servant to go and smoke a cigar with Mr Moore in the back parlour! She need not have felt so hurt, for though perhaps the first, she was not destined to be the last woman who should feel the shafts of coquetry foiled when directed against him. He looked an easy prey to the flirt. Female society was charming, female gentleness genial to him; his grave lips were capable of a very soft smile. There was sensibility at times in all his features, and in this very sensibility lay the secret of his safety. A few degrees less acute, it would have been a source of weakness and peril, but its vital keenness made it both a guide and guard. It felt the power of beauty, and then it sought beyond beauty for worth, and if no worth met its research, it withdrew from mere beauty as vacant and insufficient, withdrew unwounded and tranquil.

## CHAPTER III

I shall not insist on your entering the back parlour, reader, for its atmosphere is close. It is redolent both of tobacco and of brandy and water. Mr Moore and his bookkeeper, Steele, are both smoking there, and not cigars but pipes, while each has at his elbow a reeking tumbler of something very hot. This state of things John Henry Moore regards as the beau-ideal of comfort, and Steele, though a joined Wesleyan Methodist and an eminent class leader, is precisely of the same opinion.

# EMMA

## THE LAST SKETCH

By William Makepeace Thackeray
from the *Cornhill Magazine*, April 1860

Not many days since I went to visit a house where in former
years I had received many a friendly welcome. We went in to
the owner's – an artist's – studio. Prints, pictures, and sketches
hung on the walls as I had last seen and remembered them. The
implements of the painter's art were there. The light which had
shone upon so many, many hours of patient and cheerful toil,
poured through the northern window upon print and bust, lay
figure and sketch, and upon the easel before which the good,
the gentle, the beloved Leslie laboured. In this room the busy
brain had devised, and the skilful hand executed, I know not
how many of the noble works which have delighted the world
with their beauty and charming humour. Here the poet called
up into pictorial presence, and informed with life, grace,
beauty, infinite friendly mirth and wondrous naturalness of
expression, the people of whom his dear books told him the
stories, – his Shakespeare, his Cervantes, his Molière, his Le
Sage. There was his last work on the easel – a beautiful fresh
smiling shape of Titania, such as his sweet guileless fancy
imagined the *Midsummer Night's* queen to be. Gracious, and
pure, and bright, the sweet smiling image glimmers on the
canvas. Fairy elves, no doubt, were to have been grouped
around their mistress in laughing clusters. Honest Bottom's
grotesque head and form are indicated as reposing by the side of
the consummate beauty. The darkling forest would have grown
around them, with the stars glittering from the midsummer sky:

the flowers at the queen's feet, and the boughs and foliage about her, would have been peopled with gambolling sprites and fays. They were dwelling in the artist's mind no doubt, and would have been developed by that patient, faithful, admirable genius: but the busy brain stopped working, the skilful hand fell lifeless, the loving, honest heart ceased to beat. What was she to have been – that fair Titania – when perfected by the patient skill of the poet, who in imagination saw the sweet innocent figure, and with tender courtesy and caresses, as it were, posed and shaped and traced the fair form? Is there record kept anywhere of fancies conceived, beautiful, unborn? Some day will they assume form in some yet undeveloped light? If our bad unspoken thoughts are registered against us, and are written in the awful account, will not the good thoughts unspoken, the love and' tenderness, the pity, beauty, charity, which pass through the breast, and cause the heart to throb with silent good, find a rememberance, too? A few weeks more, and this lovely offspring of the poet's conception would have been complete – to charm the world with its beautiful mirth. May there not be some sphere unknown to us where it may have an existence? They say our words, once out of our lips, go travelling in *omne œvum*, reverberating for ever and ever. If our words, why not our thoughts? If the Has Been, why not the Might Have Been?

Some day our spirits may be permitted to walk in galleries of fancies more wondrous and beautiful than any achieved works which at present we see, and our minds to behold and delight in masterpieces which poets' and artists' minds have fathered and conceived only.

With a feeling much akin to that with which I looked upon the friend's – the admirable artist's – unfinished work, I can fancy many readers turning to these – the last pages which were traced by Charlotte Brontë's hand. Of the multitude that has read her books, who has not known and deplored the tragedy of her family, her own most sad and untimely fate? Which of her readers has not become her friend? Who that has known her books has not admired the artist's noble English, the burning love of truth, the bravery, the simplicity, the indignation at wrong, the eager sympathy, the pious love and reverence, the passionate honour, so to speak, of the woman? What a story is that of that family of poets in their solitude yonder on the gloomy northern moors! At nine o'clock at night, Mrs Gaskell tells, after evening prayers, when their guardian and relative had gone to bed, the three poetesses – the three maidens, Charlotte, and Emily, and Anne – Charlotte being the 'motherly friend and guardian to the other two' – 'began, like restless wild animals, to pace up and down their parlour, "making out" their wonderful stories, talking over plans and projects, and thoughts of what was to be their future life.'

One evening, at the close of 1854, as Charlotte Nicholls sat with her husband by the fire, listening to the howling of the wind about the house, she suddenly said to her husband, 'If you had not been with me, I must have been writing now.' She then ran upstairs, and brought down, and read aloud, the beginning of a new tale. When she had finished, her husband remarked, 'The critics will accuse you of repetition.' She replied, 'Oh! I shall alter that. I always begin two or three times before I can please myself.' But it was not to be. The trembling little hand was to write no more. The heart, newly awakened to love and happiness, and throbbing with maternal hope, was soon to cease to beat; that intrepid outspeaker and champion of truth, that eager, impetuous redresser of wrong, was to be called out of the world's fight and struggle, to lay down the shining arms, and to be removed to a sphere where even a noble indignation *cor ulterius nequit lacerare*, and where truth complete, and right triumphant, no longer need to wage war.

I can only say of this lady, *vidi tantum*. I saw her first just as I rose out of an illness from which I had never thought to recover. I remember the trembling little frame, the little hand, the great honest eyes. An impetuous honesty seemed to me to characterize the woman. Twice I recollect she took me to task for what she held to be errors in doctrine. Once about Fielding we had a disputation. She spoke her mind out. She jumped too rapidly to conclusions. (I have smiled at one or two passages in the *Biography*, in which my own disposition or behaviour forms the subject of talk.) She formed conclusions that might be wrong, and built up whole theories of character upon them.

New to the London world, she entered it with an independent, indomitable spirit of her own; and judged of contemporaries, and especially spied out arrogance or affectation, with extraordinary keenness of vision. She was angry with her favourites if their conduct or conversation fell below her ideal. Often she seemed to me to be judging the London folk prematurely: but perhaps the city is rather angry at being judged. I fancied an austere little Joan of Arc marching in upon us, and rebuking our easy lives, our easy morals. She gave me the impression of being a very pure, and lofty, and high-minded person. A great and holy reverence of right and truth seemed to be with her always. Such, in our brief interview, she appeared to me. As one thinks of that life so noble, so lonely – of that passion for truth – of those nights and nights of eager study, swarming fancies, invention, depression, elation, prayer; as one reads the necessarily incomplete, though most touching and admirable history of the heart that throbbed in this one little frame – of this one amongst the myriads of souls that have lived and died on this great earth – this great earth? – this little speck in the infinite universe of God, – with what wonder do we think of to-day, with what awe await to-morrow, when that which is now but darkly seen shall be clear! As I read this little fragmentary sketch, I think of the rest. Is it? And where is it? Will not the leaf be turned some day, and the story be told? Shall the deviser of the tale somewhere perfect the history of little EMMA'S griefs and troubles? Shall TITANIA come forth complete with her sportive court, with the flowers at her feet, the forest around her, and all the stars of summer glittering overhead?

How well I remember the delight, and wonder, and pleasure with which I read *Jane Eyre*, sent to me by an author whose name and sex were then alike unknown to me; the strange fascinations of the book; and how with my own work pressing upon me, I could not, having taken the volumes up, lay them down until they were read through! Hundreds of those who, like myself, recognized and admired that master-work of a great genius, will look with a mournful interest and regard and curiosity upon this, the last fragmentary sketch from the noble hand which wrote *Jane Eyre*.

W.M.T.

# EMMA

## (A FRAGMENT OF A STORY BY
## THE LATE CHARLOTTE BRONTË)

## CHAPTER I

We all seek an ideal in life. A pleasant fancy began to visit me in
a certain year, that perhaps the number of human beings is few
who do not find their quest at some era of life for some space
more or less brief. I had certainly not found mine in youth,
though the strong belief I held of its existence sufficed through
all my brightest and freshest time to keep me hopeful. I had not
found it in maturity. I was become resigned never to find it. I
had lived certain dim years entirely tranquil and unexpectant.
And now I was not sure but something was hovering round my
hearth which pleased me wonderfully.

Look at it, reader. Come into my parlour and judge for
yourself whether I do right to care for this thing. First, you may
scan me, if you please. We shall go on better together after a
satisfactory introduction and due apprehension of identity. My
name is Mrs Chalfont. I am a widow. My house is good, and
my income such as need not check the impulse either of charity
or a moderate hospitality. I am not young, nor yet old. There is
no silver yet in my hair, but its yellow lustre is gone. In my face
wrinkles are yet to come, but I have almost forgotten the days
when it wore any bloom. I married when I was very young. I
lived for fifteen years a life which, whatever its trials, could not
be called stagnant. Then for five years I was alone, and, having
no children, desolate. Lately Fortune, by a somewhat curious turn
of her wheel, placed in my way an interest and a companion.

The neighbourhood where I live is pleasant enough, its scenery agreeable, and its society civilized, though not numerous. About a mile from my house there is a ladies' school, established but lately – not more than three years since. The conductresses of this school were of my acquaintances; and though I cannot say that they occupied the very highest place in my opinion – for they had brought back from some months' residence abroad, for finishing purposes, a good deal that was fantastic, affected, and pretentious – yet I awarded them some portion of that respect which seems the fair due of all women who face life bravely, and try to make their own way by their own efforts.

About a year after the Misses Wilcox opened their school, when the number of their pupils was as yet exceedingly limited, and when, no doubt, they were looking out anxiously enough for augmentation, the entrance-gate to their little drive was one day thrown back to admit a carriage – 'a very handsome, fashionable carriage', Miss Mabel Wilcox said, in narrating the circumstance afterwards – and drawn by a pair of really splendid horses. The sweep up the drive, the loud ring at the door-bell, the bustling entrance into the house, the ceremonious admission to the bright drawing-room, roused excitement enough in Fuchsia Lodge. Miss Wilcox repaired to the reception-room in a pair of new gloves, and carrying in her hand a handkerchief of French cambric.

She found a gentleman seated on the sofa, who, as he rose up, appeared a tall, fine-looking personage; at least she thought him so, as he stood with his back to the light. He introduced himself as Mr Fitzgibbon, inquired if Miss Wilcox had a vacancy, and intimated that he wished to intrust to her care a new pupil in the shape of his daughter. This was welcome news, for there was many a vacancy in Miss Wilcox's schoolroom; indeed, her establishment was as yet limited to the select number of three, and she and her sisters were looking forward with anything but confidence to the balancing of accounts at the close of their first half-year. Few objects could have been more agreeable to her then, than that to which, by a wave of the hand, Mr Fitzgibbon now directed her attention – the figure of a child standing near the drawing-room window.

Had Miss Wilcox's establishment boasted fuller ranks – had she indeed entered well on that course of prosperity which in after years an undeviating attention to externals enabled her so triumphantly to realize – an early thought with her would have been to judge whether the acquisition now offered was likely to answer well as a show-pupil. She would have instantly marked her look, dress, &c., and inferred her value from these indicia. In those anxious commencing times, however, Miss Wilcox could scarce afford herself the luxury of such appreciation: a new pupil represented 40*l.* a year, independently of masters' terms – and 40*l.* a year was a sum Miss Wilcox needed and was glad to secure; besides, the fine carriage, the fine gentleman, and the fine name gave gratifying assurance, enough and to spare, of eligibility in the proffered connection. It was admitted, then, that there were vacancies in Fuchsia Lodge; that Miss Fitzgibbon could be received at once; that she was to learn all that the school prospectus proposed to teach; to be liable to every extra; in short, to be as expensive, and consequently as profitable a pupil, as any directress's heart could wish. All this was arranged as upon velvet, smoothly and liberally. Mr Fitzgibbon showed in the transaction none of the hardness of the bargain-making man of business, and as little of the penurious anxiety of the straitened professional man. Miss Wilcox felt him to be 'quite the gentleman'. Everything disposed her to be partially inclined towards the little girl whom he, on taking leave, formally committed to her guardianship; and as if no circumstance should be wanting to complete her happy impression, the address left written on a card served to fill up the measure of Miss Wilcox's satisfaction – Conway Fitzgibbon, Esq., May Park, Midland County. That very day three decrees were passed in the new-comer's favour:–

1st. That she was to be Miss Wilcox's bed-fellow.

2nd. To sit next her at table.

3rd. To walk out with her.

In a few days it became evident that a fourth secret clause had been added to these, viz. that Miss Fitzgibbon was to be favoured, petted, and screened on all possible occasions.

An ill-conditioned pupil, who before coming to Fuchsia Lodge had passed a year under the care of certain old-fashioned Misses Sterling, of Hartwood, and from them had picked up unpractical notions of justice, took it upon her to utter an opinion on this system of favouritism.

'The Misses Sterling', she injudiciously said, 'never distinguished any girl because she was richer or better dressed than the rest. They would have scorned to do so. *They* always rewarded girls according as they behaved well to their school-fellows and minded their lessons, not according to the number of their silk dresses, and fine laces and feathers.'

For it must not be forgotten that Miss Fitzgibbon's trunks, when opened, disclosed a splendid wardrobe; so fine were the various articles of apparel, indeed, that instead of assigning for their accommodation the painted deal drawers of the school bedroom, Miss Wilcox had them arranged in a mahogany bureau in her own room. With her own hands, too, she would on Sundays array the little favourite in her quilted silk pelisse, her hat and feathers, her ermine boa, and little French boots and gloves. And very self-complacent she felt when she led the young heiress (a letter from Mr Fitzgibbon, received since his first visit, had communicated the additional particulars that his daughter was his only child, and would be the inheritress of his estates, including May Park, Midland County) – when she led her, I say, into the church, and seated her stately by her side at the top of the gallery-pew. Unbiassed observers might, indeed, have wondered what there was to be proud of, and puzzled their heads to detect the special merits of this little woman in silk – for, to speak truth, Miss Fitzgibbon was far from being the beauty of the school: there were two or three blooming little faces amongst her companions lovelier than hers. Had she been a poor child, Miss Wilcox herself would not have liked her physiognomy at all: rather, indeed, would it have repelled than attracted her; and, moreover – though Miss Wilcox hardly confessed the circumstance to herself, but, on the contrary, strove hard not to be conscious of it – there were moments when she became sensible of a certain strange weariness in continuing her system of partiality. It hardly came natural to her to show this special distinction in this particular instance. An undefined wonder would smite her sometimes that she did not take more real satisfaction in flattering and caressing this embryo heiress – that she did not like better to have her always at her side, under her special charge. On principle Miss Wilcox continued the plan she had begun. On *principle*, for she argued with herself: This is the most aristocratic and richest of my pupils; she brings me the most credit and the most profit: therefore, I ought in justice to show her a special indulgence; which she did – but with a gradually increasing peculiarity of feeling.

Certainly, the undue favours showered on little Miss Fitzgibbon brought their object no real benefit. Unfitted for the character of playfellow by her position of favourite, her fellow-pupils rejected her company as decidedly as they dared. Active rejection was not long necessary; it was soon seen that passive avoidance would suffice; the pet was not social. No: even Miss Wilcox never thought her social. When she sent for her to show her fine clothes in the drawing-room when there was company, and especially when she had her into her parlour of an evening to be her own companion, Miss Wilcox used to feel curiously perplexed. She would try to talk affably to the young heiress, to draw her out, to amuse her. To herself the governess could render no reason why her efforts soon flagged; but this was invariably the case. However, Miss Wilcox was a woman of courage; and be the protégée what she might, the patroness did not fail to continue on *principle* her system of preference.

A favourite has no friends; and the observation of a gentleman, who about this time called at the Lodge and chanced to see Miss Fitzgibbon, was, 'That child looks consummately unhappy:' he was watching Miss Fitzgibbon, as she walked, by herself, fine and solitary, while her schoolfellows were merrily playing.

'Who is the miserable little wight?' he asked.

He was told her name and dignity.

'Wretched little soul!' he repeated; and he watched her pace down the walk and back again; marching upright, her hands in her ermine muff, her fine pelisse showing a gay sheen to the winter's sun, her large Leghorn hat shading such a face as fortunately had not its parallel on the premises.

'Wretched little soul!' reiterated this gentleman. He opened the drawing-room window, watched the bearer of the muff till he caught her eye, and then summoned her with his finger. She came; he stooped his head down to her; she lifted her face up to him.

'Don't you play, little girl?'

'No, sir.'

'No! why not? Do you think yourself better than other children?'

No answer.

'Is it because people tell you you are rich, you won't play?'

The young lady was gone. He stretched his hand to arrest her, but she wheeled beyond his reach, and ran quickly out of sight.

'An only child,' pleaded Miss Wilcox; 'possibly spoiled by her papa, you know; we must excuse a little pettishness.'

'Humph! I am afraid there is not a little to excuse.'

## CHAPTER II

Mr Ellin — the gentleman mentioned in the last chapter — was a man who went where he liked, and being a gossiping, leisurely person, he liked to go almost anywhere. He could not be rich, he lived so quietly; and yet he must have had some money, for, without apparent profession, he continued to keep a house and a servant. He always spoke of himself as having once been a worker; but if so, that could not have been very long since, for he still looked far from old. Sometimes of an evening, under a little social conversational excitement, he would look quite young; but he was changeable in mood, and complexion, and expression, and had chamelion eyes, sometimes blue and merry, sometimes grey and dark, and anon green and gleaming. On the

whole he might be called a fair man, of average height, rather
thin and rather wiry. He had not resided more than two years
in the present neighbourhood; his antecedents were unknown
there; but as the Rector, a man of good family and standing,
and of undoubted scrupulousness in the choice of acquaintance,
had introduced him, he found everywhere a prompt reception,
of which nothing in his conduct had yet seemed to prove him
unworthy. Some people, indeed, dubbed him 'a character', and
fancied him 'eccentric'; but others could not see the
appropriateness of the epithets. He always seemed to them very
harmless and quiet, not always perhaps so perfectly unreserved
and comprehensible as might be wished. He had a
discomposing expression in his eye; and sometimes in
conversation an ambiguous diction; but still they believed he
meant no harm.

Mr Ellin often called on the Misses Wilcox; he sometimes
took tea with them; he appeared to like tea and muffins, and
not to dislike the kind of conversation which usually
accompanies that refreshment; he was said to be a good shot,
good angler. – He proved himself an excellent gossip – he liked
gossip well. On the whole he liked women's society, and did
not seem to be particular in requiring difficult accomplishments
or rare endowments in his female acquaintance. The Misses
Wilcox, for instance, were not much less shallow than the china
saucer which held their teacups; yet Mr Ellin got on perfectly
well with them, and had apparently great pleasure in hearing
them discuss all the details of their school. He knew the names
of all their young ladies too, and would shake hands with them
if he met them walking out; he knew their examination days
and gala days, and more than once accompanied Mr Cecil, the
curate, when he went to examine in ecclesiastical history.

This ceremony took place weekly, on Wednesday afternoons,
after which Mr Cecil sometimes stayed to tea, and usually found
two or three lady parishioners invited to meet him. Mr Ellin
was also pretty sure to be there. Rumour gave one of the Misses
Wilcox in anticipated wedlock to the curate, and furnished his
friend with a second in the same tender relation; so that it is to
be conjectured they made a social, pleasant party under such

interesting circumstances. Their evenings rarely passed without Miss Fitzgibbon being introduced – all worked muslin and streaming sash and elaborated ringlets; others of the pupils would also be called in, perhaps to sing, to show off a little at the piano, or sometimes to repeat poetry. Miss Wilcox conscientiously cultivated display in her young ladies, thinking she thus fulfilled a duty to herself and to them, at once spreading her own fame and giving the children self-possessed manners.

It was curious to note how, on these occasions, good, genuine natural qualities still vindicated their superiority to counterfeit, artificial advantages. While 'dear Miss Fitzgibbon', dressed up and flattered as she was, could only sidle round the circle with the crestfallen air which seemed natural to her, just giving her hand to the guests, then almost snatching it away, and sneaking in unmannerly haste to the place allotted to her at Miss Wilcox's side, which place she filled like a piece of furniture, neither smiling nor speaking the evening through – while such was *her* deportment, certain of her companions, as Mary Franks, Jessy Newton, &c., handsome, open-countenanced little damsels – fearless because harmless – would enter with a smile of salutation and a blush of pleasure, make their pretty reverence at the drawing-room door, stretch a friendly little hand to such visitors as they knew, and sit down to the piano to play their well-practised duet with an innocent, obliging readiness which won all hearts.

There was a girl called Diana – the girl alluded to before as having once been Miss Sterling's pupil – a daring, brave girl, much loved and a little feared by her comrades. She had good faculties, both physical and mental – was clever, honest, and dauntless. In the schoolroom she set her young brow like a rock against Miss Fitzgibbon's pretensions; she found also heart and spirit to withstand them in the drawing-room. One evening, when the curate had been summoned away by some piece of duty directly after tea, and there was no stranger present but Mr Ellin, Diana had been called in to play a long, difficult piece of music which she could execute like a master. She was still in the midst of her performance, when – Mr Ellin having for the first time, perhaps, recognized the existence of the heiress by asking if she was cold – Miss Wilcox took the opportunity of launching into a strain of commendation on Miss Fitzgibbon's inanimate behaviour, terming it lady-like, modest, and exemplary. Whether Miss Wilcox's constrained tone betrayed how far she was from really feeling the approbation she expressed, how entirely she spoke from a sense of duty, and not because she felt it possible to be in any degree charmed by the personage she praised – or whether Diana, who was by nature hasty, had a sudden fit of irritability – is not quite certain, but she turned on her music-stool:–

'Ma'am,' said she to Miss Wilcox, 'that girl does not deserve so much praise. Her behaviour is not at all exemplary. In the schoolroom she is insolently distant. For my part I denounce her airs; there is not one of us but is as good or better than she, though we may not be as rich.'

And Diana shut up the piano, took her music-book under her arm, curtsied, and vanished.

Strange to relate, Miss Wilcox said not a word at the time; nor was Diana subsequently reprimanded for this outbreak. Miss Fitzgibbon had now been three months in the school, and probably the governess had had leisure to wear out her early raptures of partiality.

Indeed, as time advanced, this evil often seemed likely to right itself; again and again it seemed that Miss Fitzgibbon was about to fall to her proper level, but then, somewhat provokingly to the lovers of reason and justice, some little incident would occur to invest her insignificance with artificial interest. Once it was the arrival of a great basket of hothouse fruit – melons, grapes, and pines – as a present to Miss Wilcox in Miss Fitzgibbon's name. Whether it was that a share of these luscious productions was imparted too freely to the nominal donor, or whether she had had a surfeit of cake on Miss Mabel Wilcox's birthday, it so befel, that in some disturbed state of the digestive organs Miss Fitzgibbon took to sleep-walking. She one night terrified the school into a panic by passing through the bedrooms, all white in her night-dress, moaning and holding out her hands as she went.

Dr Percy was then sent for; his medicines, probably, did not suit the case; for within a fortnight after the somnambulistic feat, Miss Wilcox going upstairs in the dark, trod on something which she thought was the cat, and on calling for a light, found her darling Matilda Fitzgibbon curled round on the landing, blue, cold, and stiff, without any light in her half-open eyes, or any colour in her lips, or movement in her limbs. She was not soon roused from this fit; her senses seemed half scattered; and Miss Wilcox had now an undeniable excuse for keeping her all day on the drawing-room sofa, and making more of her than ever.

There comes a day of reckoning both for petted heiresses and partial governesses.

One clear winter morning, as Mr Ellin was seated at breakfast, enjoying his bachelor's easy chair and damp, fresh London newspaper, a note was brought to him marked 'private', and 'in haste'. The last injunction was vain, for William Ellin did nothing in haste − he had no haste in him; he wondered anybody should be so foolish as to hurry; life was short enough without it. He looked at the little note − three-cornered, scented, and feminine. He knew the handwriting; it came from the very lady Rumour had so often assigned him as his own. The bachelor took out a morocco case, selected from a variety of little instruments a pair of tiny scissors, cut round the seal, and read:− 'Miss Wilcox's compliments to Mr Ellin, and she should be truly glad to see him for a few minutes, if at leisure. Miss W. requires a little advice. She will reserve explanations till she sees Mr E.'

Mr Ellin very quietly finished his breakfast; then, as it was a very fine December day − hoar and crisp, but serene, and not bitter − he carefully prepared himself for the cold, took his cane, and set out. He liked the walk; the air was still; the sun not wholly ineffectual; the path firm, and but lightly powdered with snow. He made his journey as long as he could by going round through many fields, and through winding, unfrequented lanes. When there was a tree in the way conveniently placed for support, he would sometimes stop, lean his back against the trunk, fold his arms, and muse. If Rumour could have seen him, she would have affirmed that he was thinking about Miss Wilcox; perhaps when he arrives at the Lodge his demeanour will inform us whether such an idea be warranted.

At last he stands at the door and rings the bell; he is admitted, and shown into the parlour – a smaller and a more private room than the drawing-room. Miss Wilcox occupies it; she is seated at her writing-table; she rises – not without air and grace – to receive her visitor. This air and grace she learnt in France; for she was in a Parisian school for six months, and learnt there a little French, and a stock of gestures and courtesies. No: it is certainly not impossible that Mr Ellin may admire Miss Wilcox. She is not without prettiness, any more than are her sisters; and she and they are one and all smart and showy. Bright stone-blue is a colour they like in dress; a crimson bow rarely fails to be pinned on somewhere to give contrast; positive colours generally – grass greens, red violets, deep yellows – are in favour with them; all harmonies are at a discount. Many people would think Miss Wilcox, standing there in her blue merino dress and pomegranate ribbon, a very agreeable woman. She has regular features; the nose is a little sharp, the lips a little thin, good complexion, light red hair. She is very business-like, very practical; she never in her life knew a refinement of feeling or of thought; she is entirely limited, respectable, and self-satisfied. She has a cool, prominent eye; sharp and shallow pupil, unshrinking and inexpansive; pale irid; light eyelashes, light brow. Miss Wilcox is a very proper and decorous person; but she could not be delicate or modest, because she is naturally destitute of sensitiveness. Her voice, when she speaks, has no vibration; her face no expression; her manner no emotion. Blush or tremor she never knew.

'What can I do for you, Miss Wilcox?' says Mr Ellin, approaching the writing-table, and taking a chair beside it.

'Perhaps you can advise me,' was the answer; 'or perhaps you can give me some information. I feel so thoroughly puzzled, and really fear all is not right.'

'Where? and how?'

'I will have redress if it be possible,' pursued the lady; 'but how to set about obtaining it! Draw to the fire, Mr Ellin; it is a cold day.'

They both drew to the fire. She continued:–

'You know the Christmas holidays are near?'

He nodded.

'Well, about a fortnight since, I wrote, as is customary, to the friends of my pupils, notifying the day when we break up, and requesting that, if it was desired that any girl should stay the vacation, intimation should be sent accordingly. Satisfactory and prompt answers came to all the notes except one – that addressed to Conway Fitzgibbon, Esquire, May Park, Midland County – Matilda Fitzgibbon's father, you know.'

'What? won't he let her go home?'

'Let her go home, my dear sir! you shall hear. Two weeks elapsed, during which I daily expected an answer; none came. I felt annoyed at the delay, as I had particularly requested a speedy reply. This very morning I had made up my mind to write again, when – what do you think the post brought me?'

'I should like to know.'

'My own letter – actually my own – returned from the post-office, with an intimation – such an intimation! – but read for yourself.'

She handed to Mr Ellin an envelope; he took from it the returned note and a paper – the paper bore a hastily-scrawled line or two. It said, in brief terms, that there was no such place in Midland County as May Park, and that no such person had ever been heard of there as Conway Fitzgibbon, Esquire.

On reading this, Mr Ellin slightly opened his eyes.

'I hardly thought it was so bad as this,' said he.

'What? you did think it was bad then? You suspected that something was wrong?'

'Really! I scarcely knew what I thought or suspected. How very odd, no such place as May Park! The grand mansion, the grounds, the oaks, the deer, vanished clean away. And then Fitzgibbon himself! But you saw Fitzgibbon – he came in his carriage?'

'In his carriage!' echoed Miss Wilcox; 'a most stylish equipage, and himself a most distinguished person. Do you think, after all, there is some mistake?'

'Certainly, a mistake; but when it is rectified I don't think Fitzgibbon or May Park will be forthcoming. Shall I run down to Midland County and look after these two precious objects?'

'Oh! would you be so good, Mr Ellin? I knew you would be so kind; personal inquiry, you know – there's nothing like it.'

'Nothing at all. Meantime, what shall you do with the child – the pseudo-heiress, if pseudo she be? Shall you correct her – let her know her place?'

'I think,' responded Miss Wilcox, reflectively – 'I think not exactly as yet; my plan is to do nothing in a hurry; we will inquire first. If after all she should turn out to be connected as was at first supposed, one had better not do anything which one might afterwards regret. No; I shall make no difference with her till I hear from you again.'

'Very good. As you please,' said Mr Ellin, with that coolness which made him so convenient a counsellor in Miss Wilcox's opinion. In his dry laconism she found the response suited to her outer worldliness. She thought he said enough if he did not oppose her. The comment he stinted so avariciously she did not want.

Mr Ellin 'ran down,' as he said, to Midland County. It was an errand that seemed to suit him; for he had curious predilections as well as peculiar methods of his own. Any secret quest was to his taste; perhaps there was something of the amateur detective in him. He could conduct an inquiry and draw no attention. His quiet face never looked inquisitive, nor did his sleepless eye betray vigilance.

He was away about a week. The day after his return, he appeared in Miss Wilcox's presence as cool as if he had seen her but yesterday. Confronting her with that fathomless face he liked to show her, he first told her he had done nothing.

Let Mr Ellin be as enigmatical as he would, he never puzzled Miss Wilcox. She never saw enigma in the man. Some people feared, because they did not understand, him; to her it had not yet occurred to begin to spell his nature or analyze his character. If she had an impression about him, it was, that he was an idle but obliging man, not aggressive, of few words, but often convenient. Whether he were clever and deep, or deficient and

shallow, close or open, odd or ordinary, she saw no practical
end to be answered by inquiry, and therefore did not inquire.

'Why had he done nothing?' she now asked.

'Chiefly because there was nothing to do.'

'Then he could give her no information?'

'Not much: only this, indeed – Conway Fitzgibbon was a
man of straw; May Park a house of cards. There was no vestige
of such man or mansion in Midland County, or in any other
shire in England. Tradition herself had nothing to say about
either the name or the place. The Oracle of old deeds and
registers, when consulted, had not responded.'

'Who can he be, then, that came here, and who is this child?'

'That's just what I can't tell you: – an incapacity which makes
me say I have done nothing.'

'And how am I to get paid?'

'Can't tell you that either.'

'A quarter's board and education owing, and masters' terms
besides,' pursued Miss Wilcox. 'How infamous! I can't afford
the loss.'

'And if we were only in the good old times,' said Mr Ellin,
'where we ought to be, you might just send Miss Matilda out to
the plantations in Virginia, sell her for what she is worth, and
pay yourself.'

'Matilda, indeed, and Fitzgibbon! A little impostor! I wonder
what her real name is?'

'Betty Hodge? Poll Smith? Hannah Jones?' suggested Mr
Ellin.

'Now,' cried Miss Wilcox, 'give me credit for sagacity! It's
very odd, but try as I would – and I made every effort – I never
could really like that child. She has had every indulgence in this
house; and I am sure I made great sacrifice of feeling to
principle in showing her much attention; for I could not make
any one believe the degree of antipathy I have all along felt
towards her.'

'Yes. I can believe it. I saw it.'

'Did you? Well – it proves that my discernment is rarely at
fault. Her game is up now, however; and time it was. I have
said nothing to her yet; but now——'

'Have her in whilst I am here,' said Mr Ellin. 'Has she known of this business? Is she in the secret? Is she herself an accomplice, or a mere tool? Have her in.'

Miss Wilcox rang the bell, demanded Matilda Fitzgibbon, and the false heiress soon appeared. She came in her ringlets, her sash, and her furbelowed dress adornments – alas! no longer acceptable.

'Stand there!' said Miss Wilcox, sternly, checking her as she approached the hearth. 'Stand there on the farther side of the table. I have a few questions to put to you, and your business will be to answer them. And mind – let us have the truth. *We will not endure lies.*'

Every since Miss Fitzgibbon had been found in the fit, her face had retained a peculiar paleness and her eyes a dark orbit. When thus addressed, she began to shake and blanch like conscious guilt personified.

'Who are you?' demanded Miss Wilcox. 'What do you know about yourself?'

A sort of half-interjection escaped the girl's lips; it was a sound expressing partly fear, and partly the shock the nerves feel when an evil, very long expected, at last and suddenly arrives.

'Keep yourself still, and reply, if you please,' said Miss Wilcox, whom nobody should blame for lacking pity, because nature had not made her compassionate. 'What is your name? We know you have no right to that of Matilda Fitzgibbon.'

She gave no answer.

'I do insist upon a reply. Speak you shall, sooner or later. So you had better do it at once.'

This inquisition had evidently a very strong effect upon the subject of it. She stood as if palsied, trying to speak, but apparently not competent to articulate.

Miss Wilcox did not fly into a passion, but she grew very stern and urgent; spoke a little loud; and there was a dry clamour in her raised voice which seemed to beat upon the ear and bewilder the brain. Her interest had been injured – her pocket wounded – she was vindicating her rights – and she had no eye to see, and no nerve to feel, but for the point in hand. Mr Ellin appeared to consider himself strictly a looker-on; he stood on the hearth very quiet.

At last the culprit spoke. A low voice escaped her lips. 'Oh, my head!' she cried, lifting her hands to her forehead. She staggered, but caught the door and did not fall. Some accusers might have been startled by such a cry – even silenced; not so Miss Wilcox. She was neither cruel nor violent; but she was coarse, because insensible. Having just drawn breath, she went on, harsh as ever.

Mr Ellin, leaving the hearth, deliberately paced up the room as if he were tired of standing still, and would walk a little for a change. In returning and passing near the door and the criminal, a faint breath seemed to seek his ear, whispering his name –

'Oh, Mr Ellin!'

The child dropped as she apoke. A curious voice – not like Mrs Ellin's, though it came from his lips – asked Miss Wilcox to cease speaking, and say no more. He gathered from the floor what had fallen on it. She seemed overcome, but not unconscious. Resting beside Mr Ellin, in a few minutes she again drew breath. She raised her eyes to him.

'Come, my little one; have no fear,' said he.

Reposing her head against him, she gradually became reassured. It did not cost him another word to bring her round; even that strong trembling was calmed by the mere effects of his protection. He told Miss Wilcox, with remarkable tranquillity, but still with a certain decision, that the little girl must be put to bed. He carried her upstairs, and saw her laid there himself. Returning to Miss Wilcox, he said:

'Say no more to her. Beware, or you will do more mischief than you think or wish. That kind of nature is very different from yours. It is not possible that you should like it; but let it alone. We will talk more on the subject to-morrow. Let me question her.'

The Brontë Society was founded in 1893 to promote interest in the works and lives of the Brontë family. It owns and runs the Brontë Parsonage Museum at Haworth and organizes conferences, excursions and lectures. Its journal, *Transactions*, is published twice a year. Information about the society can be obtained from the membership secretary, the Brontë Society, Brontë Parsonage Museum, Haworth, Keighley, West Yorkshire, BD22 8DR.

# HELEN WITH THE HIGH HAND

## ARNOLD BENNETT

It is difficult to say who is the more delightful in this charming domestic comedy: James Ollerenshaw or high-handed Helen who arrives to disturb his miserly, measured existence.

When Helen Rathbone met her estranged step-uncle James on a park bench in one of the Five Towns, no citizen of this provincial manufacturing region could have guessed what a turn events would take, least of all the two protagonists. Helen was quite convinced she could change James Ollerenshaw for the better, whilst he was equally determined that she should not. From that moment their lives were inextricably bound together and would affect many more inside and outside their circle.

# LADY ANNA

## ANTHONY TROLLOPE

Lovel Grange was a small house, the residence of
a rich nobleman, lying among the mountains
which separate Cumberland from Westmorland,
about ten miles from Keswick. To it came
Josephine Murray as a beautiful young bride who
considered it quite the thing to be the wife of a
lord.

She had not lived with the Earl six months
before he told her that the marriage was no
marriage – she was his mistress. Her unborn child,
the Lady Anna, could make no claim to his title.
Threats were issued by the Murray family, a duel
was fought, but years of suffering were still to
come.

Their only help-mate was one Thomas Thwaite,
a tailor of Keswick, acquainted with Wordsworth
and Southey, intelligent, upstanding, impulsive and
who hated the Earl of Lovel with all his heart – had
even attacked him outside Lovel Grange. The stage
was set for high drama.